THE GIRL
WHO INVENTED
Romance

I hadn't asked Richie to love me. Just to have fun being with me.

And he couldn't bother.

I wasn't worth it.

I was crying horribly.

'You matter to me,' said Daddy.

Every father in the world, and every mother, has tried to end a talk with that line. You matter *to me*, dear. *I* love you. So what if there's not a boy on earth who does? Your old daddy loves you, and that's what counts, huh?

THE GIRL
WHO INVENTED
Romance

CAROLINE B. COONEY

Teens · Mandarin

First published in Great Britain 1991
by Teens, an imprint of Reed Consumer Books Ltd
Michelin House, 81 Fulham Road, London SW3 6RB
and Auckland, Melbourne, Singapore and Toronto
First published in the USA in 1988
by Bantam Books, Inc.

Reprinted 1993

Copyright © 1988 Caroline B. Cooney

A CIP catalogue record for this title
is available from the British Library

ISBN 0 7497 0083 1

Printed in Great Britain
by Cox & Wyman Ltd, Reading, Berks.

for Harold
who prefers the game of survival
and for his sisters
who say it's the same thing

❤ This is the story of me, Kelly Williams, and how I invented Romance—a game with a capital R.

You may think that romance has been around since the beginning of time and that a sixteen-year-old high school junior would have a very hard time inventing it.

But I did.

I even got a copyright on it, that's how good my invention was.

And how many girls can say that about romance?

But whether there were any boys in this romance—any real, loving boys who put me first—well, here's the true story.

1

❤ I was filling out a quiz in *Redbook* magazine to see if my marriage was stable.

"You're only sixteen, Kelly," said my best friend. "You don't even have a boyfriend, let alone an unstable marriage."

"That just makes it more challenging. I have to dream up a husband, work my way through five years of marriage, and analyze our relationship."

We sprawled across the pink ribcord bedspread in my room while I finished the quiz. "I got a seventy-three, Faith."

"What does seventy-three mean?"

I flipped pages. "It means my husband and I are not yet verging on divorce, but we should be aware that we have serious marital difficulties that are going to pose major problems if we don't face them right now."

I dropped the magazine on the floor and lowered my face right into the bedspread. In a minute I would have a striped face. I've been trying to destroy the ribcord all my life, so I can buy a prettier, more fragile bedspread, but nothing can damage that thing. Not dirty shoes, spilled perfume, pizza topping, or aerobic exercises.

"It makes me sad just to think about your marriage," said Faith. "You haven't even *met* this guy yet, and already your marriage is in trouble."

The magazine had fallen open to a home-decorating page. It was a bedroom for dreams: open, airy, gauzy, with no junk around (like my electric rollers, books, makeup, souvenirs, sweaters that don't fit, sweaters that do fit), and all in soft pale colors. The model in the picture was also soft and pale, but you knew that lined up outside the door were dozens of men all yearning for her. She just had that confident look.

"That confident look," said Faith, "is because she's getting paid so much. She probably doesn't have a date tonight either, Kelly."

"We should have gone to the basketball game," I said. "Then at least we'd be having fun."

"We were at basketball games Tuesday and Wednesday. How many times a week can a girl watch Will, Scott, Mario, Angie and Jeep?"

I just looked at her.

"You're right," she admitted instantly. "A girl could admire those guys every night of the week."

I turned over. The ribcord had dented my face. If we went on to the basketball game now, I'd have to wear a mask. "You know what let's do?" I said. "Let's invent a romance game."

"I'm sick of games. I want a real romance."

"Maybe one will come out of this." I had an idea. "Four of the five starters on the basketball team are in sociology class with us, right?"

"Right."

"And sociology is a forty-seven-minute stretch of time, five days a week, of total boredom, right?"

"Right."

"So let's turn the classroom into a game room. Let's make up rules and play for the boys."

"Oh, Kelly," said Faith, really annoyed with me. "Kelly, I'm not like Megan or Honey. I can't glance a boy's way and have him get all excited and flirty. What do you mean—play for the boys? I've been going in and out of crushes since I was twelve, and what do I have to show for it? Not a single date. I've read every romance book there is and every article in *Seventeen*, and what do I have junior year? Every weekend free. Now, don't let's talk about playing for the boys. I can't do it, I don't know how, and I've given up. Tomorrow I plan to hurl myself down the cellar stairs anyway."

We both giggled. It was Faith's biggest threat. Her house happens to be a ranch built on a slab. But hey. Sounds impressive.

"Who's your crush on this week?" I said. My turn to be serious. Faith is almost always in the grip of a crush. And do I mean grip. The crush seizes her, rules her life, guides her activities, and the worst of it is, the boy never notices. I take that back. Once in ninth grade the boy noticed. He fled so thoroughly, she never saw him again to keep the crush alive.

"Angie," Faith told me dreamily.

And is it ever a dream. Angie (Angelo Angelotti actually) is the beloved star of the Cummington basketball team. All five of our starters are stars, but it's hard to get excited about the stardom of Will, who is very tall, bony, and so conceited I think he may have spoken to six people in the last year, all of whom were teammates or coaches, or about the stardom of Scott, who is personality-free with the I.Q. of a cold day in January.

That leaves you with Angie, who has such a terrific time playing the game that you can't keep your eyes off him (you wouldn't keep your eyes off him anyway, because he's so totally cute) and with Jeep (real name George Peters, initials G.P., leads to Jeep), who is centerfold material: handsome like a soap-opera star, with strong, memorable features, thick windblown dark hair, and soft sad dark eyes.

I forgot Mario.

Everybody forgets Mario. I'm sure nobody ever had a crush on him. He gets almost as many points as Will, but Will is at least so tall, you can distinguish him from anybody else. Mario is just sort of there. This is probably the last time I'll ever need to mention Mario.

Anyway, if Faith had a crush on Angie, she was standing in line with a lot of other girls, and Angie has never been known to date a girl twice.

"There are eleven boys in sociology class," I said to Faith. "Of whom three are basketball stars, right? Will, Jeep, and Angie, right?"

"Right. And two are Stephen and Alan, who are both going extremely steady. And two are Avery and Kenny who are both extremely total losers. And two are—"

"Be quiet. I'm planning the game. Don't interrupt me."

Faith rolled her eyes. She got off the bed, wandered around my room, and landed in front of my fingernail-polish collection. Last Christmas both my grandmothers, my aunt Suzanne, and my next-door neighbor I baby-sit for gave me enormous gift sets of nail polish. I could practically go into retail right off my dresser. "Can I try the silver decals on the Wineblush Frost?" said Faith.

"You may *have* the silver decals and the Wineblush

Frost. Here's how the game will go, Faith. I've worked it out in my mind. We'll walk into sociology Monday, right?"

"I'm with you. We're walking into sociology."

"And there are eleven boys there, right?"

"If you're counting Chuckie, who in my opinion does not qualify for either gender."

"I'm counting Chuckie. I know he's a boy because he's in boys' gym."

"Good clue."

"Okay. It's a game of chance."

"I hate chance," said Faith. "I like skill."

"If we had any skill," I pointed out, "we'd be off somewhere tonight with the boys of our choice."

"Good point." Faith put Wineblush Frost on her left hand with precision. Faith's hands never quiver. Mine always do, and my nails have a sticky, confused look. When even your fingernails are confused, you know you're in trouble.

"Okay. We have to select a boy on whom to work. The selection will be by chance."

Faith shuddered. "If chance gives me Chuckie, or Avery, or Kenny, I'll leave town."

"Keep your fingers crossed. Maybe you'll get Angie."

Faith started to tell me about how wonderful Angie was, but I knew that as well as she did, it would be boring conversation. If she went and had a crush on, say, Kenny, who belongs on zoo-cleanup detail, it would be interesting. Sickening. Humiliating. But interesting.

I interrupted her. "We'll figure out some kind of countdown that we can't know until class begins. Then we'll do some sort of Eenie, Meenie, Minie, Mo and find out who each plays the game with."

"But what's the game?"

7

"I haven't figured that out yet. Don't rush me. We creative types need time in which to flower."

"If we're going to spend *that* much time," said Faith, who, when it comes to me, does not have as much faith as I would like, "I'll get out the Monopoly game because we're going to be up till dawn anyhow."

"Laugh," I told her. "You'll regret it when you're left out."

Faith finished her right hand and stuck the Wineblush Frost in her purse. She began peeling tiny silver decals and placing them diagonally on her long, perfect nails. Faith is very pretty in a sweet, plump way. Plump is an exaggeration. She's a little thick in the waist. It's just that I'm so thin, I get carried away about other people's figures. I'm not thin-attractive—willowy, slender, fragile-thin. I'm thin-*scary,* so that other people's mothers are always muttering in under-tones, "Does she have anorexia?" "No, Mother, she's always been like that." "Are you sure? She looks one foot in the grave to me." "No, Mother, Kelly's shaped like a pencil. There's nothing she can do about it." "She could try eating."

"Okay, here's the plan. We get our boy. Then we have to start following steps, like the squares on a Monopoly board, to attract him."

"If it's Angie, I like it. If it's Kenny, pardon me while I gag."

"Just gag over the ribcord, will you? I'm trying to ruin it."

"Nothing will ever ruin it. You will give it in perfect condition to your grandchildren."

"Now, there's a happy thought," I said. "It implies that I'm going to get married one day, which means I will surely go out with at least one boy."

"You won't be so happy if you draw Kenny."

"Okay. We're going to take dice into class. The first number we roll is the vertical seat row. The second number we roll is the seat within the row. That's the boy we get."

"Except what if we roll a girl?" said Faith.

I had forgotten about girls. There were quite a few in sociology too.

"We'll come back to that," said Faith kindly. "Get to the good part. What are the moves?"

I tapped my palm with a pencil. I always think better with a pencil. It's a problem in computer class. I have to hold the thinking pencil in my teeth.

"Square one," I said, reflecting on every magazine quiz, self-help article, and lovelorn letter I ever read. (Thousands. Possibly millions. And how improved *am* I? Maybe I should ask for my money back on all those issues.) "First move is, you have to smile at him."

"I can handle that," said Faith. "I got my braces off and I have new lipstick."

"Square two. *Notice* him."

"You said that very intensely, Kelly. In what way are we supposed to *notice* him?"

"Absorb every detail. Be terribly aware. Soak it up."

"Why?"

"Future reference."

"Okay. Square two. I'm noticing him," agreed Faith. "Now, what's square three?"

"Talk to him."

"Does this have to be in public? Because if I land on Kenny, I'd rather get typhoid."

"It has to be in public. Everything has to be in public. That way we'll develop poise."

"I doubt it," said Faith. "This already sounds like something a twelve-year-old would do, and we're sixteen. I think you and I may be a little low in the poise department."

"You have no faith," I accused her.

Faith just looked at me again. She didn't need to say what she was thinking now. She detested her name. She feels that F names are frowsy and fat. If she were Jody, say, or Laurie— now those are names Romance can take and run with. But Faith? Frumpy. Solid. Sturdy.

"Square four," I said, "will be *sit next to him*."

Now we were at the tricky part.

Because although we do not have assigned seats in sociology (or anywhere else except study hall, where there are so many of us, they don't check us off by name, but by position on the grid, and you'd better believe *that* leads to a lot of cutting and cover-ups) nevertheless, people tend to sit in the same place every day.

There are some who have to be in the back row, and some who need a window. Some who can't see the blackboard unless they're up front, and some who have to sit next to their best friend or die, and so forth.

Sociology class is not full—I think there are nineteen or twenty of us—so there are several extra desks, but they're always empty. The same ones. If Faith and I suddenly shifted into one, people would get all confused. And if we took somebody else's seat, people would get all irritable. And what would we say in explanation? "Oh, I'm just in square four, don't worry about a thing."

"Hmm," said Faith.

"You are willing to do anything for Angie, aren't you?" I coaxed.

"Yes, but this is a game of chance. If I get a gender-free Chuckie or a megaloser Kenny, the only thing I'm willing to do for them is hide their photographs from the yearbook editor."

It was at this point that my bedroom door was flung open, hard enough that the handle dented the wall, and Megan came in sobbing, and my life changed.

Megan didn't come in with that purpose in mind. She came in hoping to change *her* life. (Actually she wanted to change her boyfriend Jimmy's life: she wanted him dead, which is as major a change as most of us will ever encounter, but she was *pretending* she wanted to change *her* life.)

"He dumped me," said Megan dramatically, shaking so hard with sobs that her tears spattered on Faith and me.

"Have a seat," said Faith, patting the bed.

Megan, Faith, and I have shared things forever. That's the trouble with living in a development. All of our parents bought new houses in Fox Meadow when we were babies. There was never a meadow, let alone any foxes, but there were supposed to be a hundred houses. Something went wrong, and they built only eighteen. I've known every family in Fox Meadow intimately since nursery school. When I was little, I loved it. If your mother didn't have any good snacks around, you could always wander through Megan's kitchen or Faith's kitchen. And if Faith's mother wouldn't let her watch television, there was sure to be one on in the Smiths' family room, and Mrs. Smith had so many little kids, she never noticed one more or less in front of the tube.

But now that I am sixteen, I would rather not live in Fox Meadow. I am tired of knowing all about everybody, and I am tired of them knowing all about me (Mrs. Smith, for example, saying, "Since you're always free on Saturday nights, Kelly, can I sign you up to baby-sit for the next two months?"), and I am very, very, very tired of Megan landing on me whenever she needs company without even knocking at the front door, let alone my bedroom door.

"He dumped me," she repeated tragically. "I *hate* that

11

word *dump.* Can't you just see it? This obscene pile of refuse, heaped by massive trucks right up to the sky, sea gulls circling overhead like small white vultures, and me, lying on top. *Dumped.*"

Megan always has dates.

In fourth grade, when the rest of us hadn't even gotten our braces *on,* let alone *off,* Megan was holding hands with Ricky out on the playground. I remember we'd say, "Eeeeuuuuh, Megan, you're sick! Why do you want to touch a *boy*?"

So it was hard to be very sympathetic about Jimmy. Next weekend she'd just go out with somebody else. Megan had an inexhaustible fund of boys. I could never figure out where she met them, let alone how she attracted them.

"For a girl he met bowling," said Megan. "It makes me quite ill. Bowling. It has no status. He could at least dump me for a girl he met skiing. Hand me your Kleenex."

I knew then that Faith and I would never mention my silly little romance game. Not with Megan and her ten hundred previous dates sitting on the bed with us. I looked down into the open Monopoly game box. There were extra dice there. I might just take one and play my silly game by myself.

"You know what I want?" said Megan, sniffing.

Presumably Jimmy.

"I want an affair like your mother's."

I was outraged. "My mother is not having an affair."

"The affair she's having with your *father,* dummy. I never come here but that he's just bought your mother chocolate, or a bouquet of violets, or a special card. And how long have they been married? Forever. Longer than any of us have even been alive."

"I should hope so," I said grumpily.

I dislike talking about my parents' romance. It's very

beautiful, and I love seeing them: They're forty and still setting the standard by which everybody in Fox Meadow goes—notes to each other tucked under the windshield wipers, the special silver charm, the perfect surprise. But it's hard to live in a house that is wall-to-wall romance and not be able to participate one single red rose worth. My older brother, Parker, literally closes his eyes whenever they get romantic. I used to think it embarrassed him, but now I think he's disgusted by it. I don't know why. Maybe he thinks they're too old and too married.

But then Parker himself is such a mystery to me right now that who knows?

Because my brother, Parker, is dating Wendy Newcombe. Wendy is the Queen of Romance: exquisitely pretty, very funny, terribly smart. She writes a daily soap opera we listen to after the principal's announcements. She dates only princes. Like Jeep.

Now, Parker is nice—in fact, *very* nice. When he graduated from junior high he was voted Nicest Boy, and I don't think anybody would change his vote four years later. But what kind of adjective is *nice*? You can't call Parker dramatic, or romantic, or handsome. He's my brother and I love him—everybody loves him—but Wendy dumped Jeep for my brother Parker, and that's amazing.

Jeep has about eight hundred wonderful qualities, from sexy to sweet, from athletic to gorgeous. Park has one wonderful quality. You wonder what Wendy was thinking of to make that trade.

Whatever it is, she's thinking of it constantly.

You should see Wendy follow Parker around. She runs the long way through the corridors between classes just to catch a glimpse of my brother going into chem lab. Last week in sociology she actually forgot to take a test, and when

13

Miss Simms asked, "Wendy, you're not taking the test?" Wendy said, "Oh, my goodness! Oh, dear!" and blushed and added, "I guess I was thinking about Parker."

Poor Jeep. He cringed. He has very good features for cringing. Actually I prefer to imagine his features in terms of kissing and serenading, but I can think of no time I would put Parker's features ahead of Jeep's. Even though he's my brother and I'm very loyal. Well, sort of loyal. Sometimes I think romance is a mystical game. You've been dealt cards you don't know what to do with. You play by rules nobody else seems to be following because they were given a different set. Or maybe, like me, you don't play at all: You can't seem to toss the right combination to start the plays.

"Oh, well," said Megan, mopping up the last of her tears and throwing Jimmy out with her Kleenex. "Let's play Monopoly. I'll be banker. Next to boys I like money best." She said "oh, well" with the reverse inflection I use: Instead of sinking with despair, her voice lifted cheerily, as if her "Oh, well" were looking forward to a new day.

"I'll be the iron," said Faith, choosing her player.

"I'll be the Scottie dog," said Megan, choosing hers.

The phone rang.

I keep my telephone under the bed because there's so much essential junk on my bedside table, the phone doesn't fit. I leaned over backward, so my vertebrae made splintering noises, and reached under. My hair, which is absolutely straight and very thin, like my body, fell around me like a silvery-gold waterfall and splashed on the carpet. About the only thing I really like about me is the color of my hair: yellow silk ribbons.

My spine crunched against the bedrails. "Hello?"

"Hello, Kelly? It's Wendy. Wendy Newcombe?"

The star of Cummington High has been dating my

brother for three months, and she thinks I don't know who she is? "Hi, Wendy. He isn't home. He's at play practice." He's stage manager of the school production of *The Music Man*. Wendy doesn't like this. She wants Park to take her to the basketball games. Parker doesn't like that, because she might be going in order to compare him to Jeep, who is out there showing off, racking up baskets and generally being a top-notch jock.

"Oh," said Wendy sadly. "I thought he'd be home by now."

Wendy's voice is very expressive. I had to bite my lips to keep from offering to run over and stay with her until Park got back. "Shall I give him a message?" I said. "Is something wrong?"

"No," said Wendy, all forlorn, like a little girl who's lost her mother in the crowd. "I just wanted to talk. No subject. Just . . . to hear his voice."

Wendy Newcombe, Queen of Romance, so in love with my brother, Parker, she just had to hear his voice.

What if I never got a phone call from a boy who just had to hear my voice? What if the only tears I ever shed were not from love—but from lack of it?

"What's the matter, Kell?" said Faith. "You stuck under there?" She and Megan yanked me up, and I shrieked to cover the sounds of my backbone twisting, and the despair I was afraid might show on my face.

We arranged ourselves cross-legged around the Monopoly board, spread in the middle of my mattress, and put props under the board so it would lie evenly and the players and cards wouldn't slide down onto our toes. I chose the top hat and looked at the familiar squares. Railroads, utilities . . .

"Don't you wish there were boys on these squares?" I

15

said. "You wouldn't buy properties, you'd get boys. You wouldn't win dollars, you'd win dates."

"I don't think there is a board game like that," said Megan.

"But if there were, I would buy it," said Faith. She put three players at GO.

"I have poster board," I said. "We could copy out the squares but put boys where the streets are. Like here." I named the powder blue squares facing me. "We could put Angie and Jeep and Will on Connecticut, Vermont, and Oriental."

Megan and Faith didn't even bother to listen. Megan took the first turn. (Megan *always* takes the first turn, and I am always annoyed, and I have never said anything.)

I didn't say anything this time either except, "I can't find my poster board. I'm going to cut typing paper into squares instead."

I Scotch-taped boy squares over the streets and penciled little cartoons of the basketball starters on them. I wrote their names in what was supposed to be romantic script, but was actually just messy handwriting.

"You're going to ruin the Monopoly board," complained Megan. "When you peel that junk off, you'll tear the whole surface."

"They have to have values," I said. "Like properties. But not dollars. Let's give all the boys a numerical rating. One to ten." I stuck Mario and Scott on Ventnor Avenue and Marvin Gardens.

"Jeep's a ten," said Megan.

"No," said Faith instantly. "Angie's the ten. There cannot be more than one ten in the game, and it has to go to Angie."

"Jeep is more handsome," said Megan.

16

"Angie is more wonderful." Faith wrote ten under his sketch.

Megan glared at us both. "You can't have a board game with a boy named Angie anyhow. Not everybody in America lives in a town that's half Italian. They don't even know that boys can have names like Angelo. Like when I lived in Miami, I knew a boy named Jesus. He was cute too. But you can't run around putting Jesus on your list of romantic boys."

I sighed. "Let's not worry about everybody in America. Let's just make the game for us."

"Think big," said Megan. "Market it nationally."

Market it.

I snorted.

"Let's not use names from the team," said Faith. "Let's pick out romantic names." Faith smiled happily, remembering romance-book plots and heroes who swung their women up on horses and took them to exotic locales and sometimes rescued them from danger. "Dirk," said Faith. "Lance. Brandon. Nicholas." She batted her eyelashes. Faith has wonderful eyes: very large, sunk so there's lots of room for various shades of eye shadow, and long, naturally dark lashes that sweep her cheeks just like a romance book-cover heroine's. That ought to make up for being plump, don't you think?"

"Real people," said Megan scornfully, "are not named Dirk. Let's go all-American: David. Charles. Michael."

I know a dozen Michaels, and I never tire of the name. I think it's beautiful. I added another square to the Monopoly board and called it Michael. I gave him a nine rating. What the heck. Might as well have high stakes, right?

"Stephen," continued Megan, making squares of her own now. "Paul. Mark. Eric. Stanley."

"Stanley?" Faith and I demanded.

17

"I used to have a cat named Stanley."

"Stanley is not a romantic name," said Faith. "I refuse to have Stanley on the board. With my luck I'd win Stanley and you'd get Lance."

Megan threw her Scottie dog at Faith. Faith flung her iron at Megan. "What are you two doing?" I yelled. "Fighting over Stanley? Stanley doesn't even exist."

"Sorry," said Megan, handing the players back to Faith to put at GO. "I was just getting excited. I always react that way to boys." She started counting out money.

"We're not going to buy the boys," said Faith.

"No, but we'll need cash for our dates."

I stared at my Monopoly board.

The solid square of utilities and avenues shifted position and condensed, getting softer, rounder. My eyes slid out of focus. The game board shouldn't be a square. A heart instead.

Perhaps a series of interlocking hearts.

GO TO JAIL turned to lace and love.

INCOME TAX became holding hands and candlelight.

PENNSYLVANIA RAILROAD was flowers and chocolates.

"Romance," I whispered.

Now I saw the lettering on the game: curlicues of gothic script with hearts and flowers entwined. Initials in trees. Notes under pillows. "We'll invent Romance: The Game of Love," I said softly. It would be pink. Several shades of pink: gentle and rosy, like the dawn of love. Perhaps the board itself would be scented.

"I don't know," said Megan, looking down at the very same board. "I kind of think this is stupid actually. I'd rather play Monopoly, where at least you know what you're after. With boys, who knows? And we can't invent a board game. How would you win? How would you know when you got to the end? And *what* would you win?"

18

What would you win?

The real board was a mishmash of chopped paper, bad drawings, and Scotch tape. In my mind it was laced with romance.

"I think I'm going home," said Megan. "I may call up Jimmy and yell at him till I feel better."

Faith got up too. "I'm sort of tired myself. I'll see you tomorrow, Kelly, okay?" She stretched, yawned, and stretched again. She started to put away the game for me, but I put my fingertips on the board and held it to the ribcord. I was still thinking.

They had become bored as fast as they'd gotten interested. But that was because I didn't have a game yet—just an idea. They couldn't go far on ideas; they had to have the real thing.

But maybe I could give it to them.

ROMANCE: The Game of Love.

And what would you win?

What does anybody want to win?

Happily Ever After.

2

♥ Miss Simms stood in front of sociology in her usual peculiar posture: left hand cupped beneath her right elbow, so her right arm is propped toward the ceiling. In this hand she holds her lecture notes, precisely angled to block the class from seeing her face.

Angie muttered, "Not that I blame her. I just wish I could block out her voice as well." Poor Miss Simms has a voice pitched too high. She sounds like a six-year-old, but she's about my parents' age and quite hefty. Even after all these months of sociology lectures, I'm startled when that squeaking voice emerges from her massive chest.

"She's not that bad, Angie," whispered Faith. Faith likes everybody.

Angie rolled his dark eyes. "She's too intense for me. I like laid-back people."

Our row has Wendy, empty seat, me, Faith, and Angie, sitting from the door to the windows. Faith sits with her knees turned to the window so she can watch Angie all period long. She's pretty obvious about it. Angie never notices.

Miss Simms lowered her cupped elbow fractionally and peered around the class. "Angelo?" she said screechingly. "Is that you talking while I am lecturing?"

Angie is one of those people with the perfect name: like a policeman named Copp or a surgeon named Cutter. He is the angel of his first and last names. With the smile of a cherub he said, "I'm sorry, Miss Simms." The smile had its usual effect. Miss Simms raised her elbow and vanished behind her notes again. Faith sighed longingly.

"I am opposed to people who call me Angelo," murmured Angie, more or less in Faith's direction. "I wish I had a real name."

Faith was close enough to touch his tight dark curls. I could tell how much she wanted to. "How about Dirk?" she suggested. "Or Lance?"

Angie lit up. "Dirk," he breathed. "It's me. Can't you see me on my mission impossible, screwing the silencer on my gun as I prepare to vanquish the enemy?"

"I see you perfectly," Faith said. "Next to you is a beautiful blonde filled with adoration."

Angie put a tough but carefree expression on his face and began scanning a distant horizon for possible national enemies. Faith choked back a giggle. Angie continued performing for her. She had certainly overdosed on romance books if she was telling Angie to have a beautiful blonde next to him. Faith was a brunette.

I had a single die in my purse. I hadn't told Faith, who had certainly forgotten about our original little romance game. But I had not forgotten. Sociology was the perfect setting. Sweet, oblivious Angie. Terrific Jeep. Conceited Will.

21

Gender-free Chuckie. Losers Kenny and Avery. Various ordinary types to fill the other squares.

The game would be my own personal indoor activity.

Playable only during sociology.

A secret.

Unless, of course, I rolled Jeep, and won the plays on the squares, and Jeep asked me out, and Wendy got jealous, and *I* was the Queen of Romance. *Then* I wouldn't keep it a secret. I would laugh, and toss my gold-ribbon hair, and know I had really won the blue.

Miss Simms was talking about quizzes.

We were going to have to design one for each other to take. Another of her weird weekend assignments. "Statistically correct," she said. "Data interpreted in a reasonable fashion. Controls that can be measured."

Nobody was listening to her. That's what sociology is at Cummington High—a forty-seven minute stretch of not listening. That's why it was a perfect place for my romance game.

"I like this, Faith," said Angie. "I'll even let you sit with me at lunch if you'll tell me more about Dirk and my beautiful blonde."

Across the empty desk next to me Wendy was perking up. Wendy rarely participates in sociology because she despises Miss Simms. But she's always on the lookout for material for her soap opera. That is what she tells Parker. "Material," she says intensely. "Let's go find material." Then they vanish for three hours in Mother's car. At night. My father mutters, "I bet I know what kind of material they're finding, all right." "Don't tell me about it," says my mother, who is of the old school of parenting: What you don't know can't hurt you. My mother is a great believer in wrapping yourself in cotton wool. Not that she ever has to wrap herself. My father is a great believer in protecting her. He provides the cotton wool, she shrinks inside it, and they're both happy.

I felt around in my purse for the die.

"And your quiz may be on any subject whatsoever," said Miss Simms, "but it must have questions each one of us in the classroom can answer. We will compile responses and get a clear profile of our own classroom."

"Anything whatsoever?" repeated Will. "Like, how many of us eat imported chocolate? Which of us are abused by our parents?"

Everybody but Faith laughed. She was too busy being thrilled about sitting with Angie at lunch. I was pretty thrilled for her. It was romantic: naming a romance name, and winning the best boy—the one you've always yearned for. I couldn't quite believe it. Neither could Wendy, who was leaning forward to catch whatever Angie was saying next to Faith.

"Those are excellent suggestions, Will!" cried Miss Simms breathlessly. She was so excited, she lowered her elbow. "A series of questions designed to glean statistics on child abuse right in our room! Now that will be meaningful!"

"Some of us might decline to answer," Jeep pointed out.

Will laughed. "Then we'll all know that under your sweatshirt, you're covered with bruises."

Jeep grinned and Will grinned back—probably the only time all week Will would do that. Normal emotions all come second to conceit in Will. "I am covered with bruises," he said. "It's my fellow basketball players. They beat up on me. I've been meaning to report it to the proper authorities, but Will keeps paying them off." Will's grin had smoothed out his face. Now he was just very bony, and very snobbish. If he ever grinned at me the way he had at Jeep, I'd know I possessed a million dollars that Will needed in five minutes.

I rolled the die gently on the desk.

It rolled off onto the floor, making a tiny clatter, like an electric typewriter, and rolled two desks away. I couldn't believe it. One limp toss and the dumb thing was gone forever. Under Will's desk.

Will heard the faint rattle, frowned slightly, and bent over to retrieve it.

He looked around to see where it had come from. When Miss Simms wasn't looking, I signaled him. Will narrowed his eyes at me. I nodded *Yes, that's really mine, yes, I want it back.* Will got up, walked two paces and handed it back.

"Will?" said Miss Simms.

"Just giving Kelly back her dice," said Will.

"Oh," said Miss Simms.

"I want to do chocolate," said Faith quickly. "My quiz will establish how many of us will kill for chocolate."

"Faith, you'll need twenty questions on your quiz. Limiting yourself to chocolate could pose problems. Perhaps you could expand your questionnaire to include—oh, say—food allergies from which we all suffer."

Angie clutched his heart with excitement. "That does sound intriguing, Miss Simms!" he cried. "I can hardly wait to find out who gets hives."

Faith lowered her fine lashes at him. "I do. Every time I think about you, Angie, I get a rash."

The class howled with laughter.

Wendy was writing it all down. Before long we would hear this dialogue over the P.A. system. Not everybody in class would recognize themselves because Wendy is pretty clever at disguising lines. But it wouldn't be strictly original. (That's the sort of thing I comfort myself with when I think that Wendy is about four hundred times more creative than I am, and I should probably give up right now.)

This time I rolled the die very, very, very gently, and quickly lowered my arms to make little walls to catch it if it tried anything sneaky.

It was a four.

I glanced over to vertical row four.

Kenny, Will, Angie, Margaret, and Susan.

So if I rolled a six next, I'd have to start over. There was no sixth seat. And if I rolled a four or five, ditto. I was not going to play my indoor game of romance with a girl. Even though I quite like Margaret, and Susan has a nice car.

Actually the other three were a good representation of the class. One totally disgusting loser. One conceited overly tall starship. And one perfect person my best friend was having lunch with. Hey, great. Just like life, huh?

I rolled again.

For a moment I didn't want to look at it. I giggled softly to myself instead. It's a habit I'm aware of, and I try to stop myself because I know how odd I must look: Kelly entertained by nothing at all. Laughing into thin air like somebody due for a long stay at a mental hospital.

I glanced around to see if anybody had spotted me laughing. Everybody but Will was laughing over Angie and Faith and the rash. "Me Dirk," said Angie broadly. "You Jane." Will was staring at me as if he rarely came across a girl so peculiar. I smiled at him. He looked away.

I lowered my eyes, my eyes landed on the die, and there were two little black dots staring at me.

Two.

Will was two.

Impossible not to laugh again. Impossible not to look at Will, who was so unlikely ever to have a romance with me. So I smiled again, realizing even as the smile touched my lips that that was square one of my own game design. *Smile at him.*

25

Will smiled back.

A real smile.

Just as if he were a real human being, and not a tall thin piece of cardboard labeled CONCEIT.

I ducked my head. My hair fell forward, slippery and straight, hiding me from everyone including Will.

You're turning chicken, I told myself. Hiding is not on one of your squares. You still have to notice him, talk to him and sit next to him.

But in the grand old tradition of school, I was saved by the bell. Basketball players charged out as if they were on a court. Wendy said, in a high, attention-getting voice, "I think that's at least two episodes, don't you?"

♥

In study hall I thought about Miss Simms's assignment. Food-allergy quizzes. Child-abuse quizzes.

Bor—ing.

Let them have their rashes and their bruises. I would take Love. I would do a romance quiz. After all, I hadn't thought about a single thing except Romance since I folded up my Monopoly game and began drawing interlocking hearts on the poster board I finally located behind my bureau.

So far I had a Start Heart, three Dating Hearts, and a Happily-Ever-After Heart.

At first I tried to define Happily Ever After, but I gave up fast. Who knows what Happily Ever After means to somebody else? A mate for your cruise around the world on your yacht? A partner for earning your first million? A companion to walk through flowery meadows with you? I would just leave Happily Ever After blank.

Okay. A romance quiz. Get on it, Kelly, I ordered myself. How about pairs? Circle which is most romantic: Roses or dandelions. Satin or denim. Motorcycles or station wagons.

But that turned out to be as boring as food allergies. Anybody would check off satin before denim. I needed a quiz that would force people to think. I began listing words.

Stars. Dark eyes. Snuggling. Earrings. Perfume. Midnight-blue. City skyline. September.

Those were fairly romantic. Words for the cover of a thick historical novel, or the backdrop of a slick magazine advertisement.

So now I needed some words that weren't romantic.

Smoking. Tacos. Compost.

And some that weren't much of anything.

Forests. Rhythm. Novels.

Maybe you'd give each word a numerical rating. One to ten. Which words were most likely to make a person think of romance? And the person taking the quiz would check off *boy* or *girl*. Maybe some words meant more to boys than they did to girls.

From study hall I went on to my last class of the day, which is American history. It was January, so we had passed the Civil War and were steaming on toward the Last Frontier, whatever that was. I had not read the chapter.

Once my mother told me if I put one tenth the effort into school that I put into complaining about not knowing any gorgeous boys, I'd at least be able to go to a good college, where there are lots of good boys to put an effort into. She's right, of course. The thing is, I can't seem to get into studying. It lacks a certain something.

Boys, I guess.

I know I could study with some terrific boy sharing the desk.

Oh, well.

Faith sat down next to me. She was so deep in her crush on Angie, she could hardly focus. Toothpaste was never marketed by a wider, whiter smile than Faith gave me as she dropped her history text onto the desk. "Kelly," she whispered.

"Yes, Faith." I have sat with her through many an agonizing crush. I estimate Faith runs about four serious crushes a year. They all hurt so much. It's so unfair that love, of all things, can be so painful.

"Do you think he'll ask me out, Kelly? Lunch was so great! We just laughed steadily. I mean, he'll *have* to want to do that again, won't he?"

Fluffy brown hair circled her eager face: a face that made the rest of us happy, a smile you had to reflect with your own. A sweet person, a good person. Had Angie seen this?

Faith shook her head twice, denying the possibility, and then nodded a couple of times, believing that it really might happen.

"Got a twitch, Faith?" said Will, striding to his seat without waiting for an answer. We didn't answer him either. From experience we knew he wouldn't be looking our way again because he didn't intend to talk to us anyhow. He just meant to demonstrate his superiority with a wisecrack and then ignore us.

What if Angie does ask Faith out? I thought. I will be the very last girl without a boyfriend. Like gym, when they're picking teams. I'll be the one still sitting on the floor while everybody pities me and nobody wants me.

"The sun is in my eyes," I croaked. "I'm changing seats." There was, in fact, a faint glint over by the windows. But the move was to get control of myself because jealousy was forming. I had to destroy it before it arrived. I refuse to feel jealousy toward my best friend.

I slid into the empty seat.

Will looked up, startled.

Without planning it, I'd arrived at square two. *Sit next to him.*

I looked quickly away. Mrs. Weston wasn't saying anything interesting, so I opened my latest magazine underneath my textbook and flipped it open to the quiz. (I don't subscribe to a magazine unless it has quizzes. I love to fill things out.)

Test your intimacy quotient, it said.

Oh, good. I always wondered what my intimacy quotient was.

1. You want to spend an afternoon with Jeff. Will you suggest
    a. Frisbee tossing?
    b. looking at his baby pictures?
    c. making fudge?
    d. shopping at the mall?
2. He isn't paying enough attention to you. Do you decide that
    a. he's too worried about his SATs?
    b. he likes another girl more?
    c. he's gay?
    d. he's getting the flu?
3. You just aren't close enough to the boy you love. Is it because
    a. he isn't your perfect ideal?
    b. you're afraid of intimacy?
    c. you can't relax with boys?
    d. he isn't fond enough of you to bother?

Dumb, dumb. I'd never do *anything* listed under the first question. As far as the second, I'd consider them all. Ditto the third.

I concentrated. Okay. Making fudge.

Mrs. Weston was talking. I tested my intimacy quotient on all twenty questions. My score was forty-seven. I looked that up.

Under 50, it said. *You have real problems relating to boys. Perhaps you should consider counseling.*

Counseling!

I didn't need a mental-health expert. I needed a boy to love me.

But even though I knew the quiz was stupid, and the questions were stupid, and the score was stupid, and even though I was in public, I started crying.

Inside myself I froze, turning the tears solid, getting very still. I won't cry, I won't cry, I won't cry.

But I couldn't help myself, and a few tears trickled down my cheeks.

A large hand with freakishly long, large fingers, landed on my magazine. Surely Mrs. Weston didn't have hands that big! Surely— But it was Will. Huge fingers curled the magazine into a cylinder (something that would take two hands for me to do) and removed it to his desk. Without unwrapping the magazine, he read the quiz, turning the roll like an axle to read the columns.

"What's your score?" Will breathed.

I considered lying. I considered not answering him at all. But Will wasn't worth it. "Forty-seven," I told him.

Will grinned. Ear to ear. He didn't bother to face me. I only saw the grin in profile.

That's right, you creep, I thought. Laugh at me. I bet you didn't get any hundred either. I bet you got a thirty-three. The only thing you've ever been intimate with is a basketball.

A low intimacy quotient.

What a thing to have in common.

The need to cry vanished, and I simply felt thick and dull. The smile faded from Will's face. He returned the magazine. He didn't tell me his score and I didn't ask.

I swiveled in my chair to see what Faith was making of my exchanges with Will.

Faith had not noticed a thing

She had written *Faith Bennett Angelotti* six times in different scripts.

Ay, boys. They may think this is the liberated eighties, but they're wrong. We're still here shading our writing with our hands so nobody can see we're trying out a boy's last name in case we should get married.

Ding, dong, ding.

Our final announcements come on, complete with chords. Mrs. Weston finished up her lecture while the principal cleared his throat, and school was over.

Our principal reads off a paper his secretary has typed for him. Unfortunately his voice stops at the end of the line whether the sentence stops there or not. Drives you crazy.

"Drives me crazy," said Will, echoing my thought. Probably the highest intimacy level I would reach all week. "Someday I'm going to put my fist through the loudspeaker," he said. But he wasn't talking to me, or to anybody. He just spoke out loud. You didn't get a thirty-three, I thought meanly, you got a zero.

"Put your fist through Dr. Schneider instead," advised somebody. "He deserves it more."

"Key Club will meet after school in order to discuss," said Dr. Schneider. He cleared his throat. We all twitched. "The fund-raiser for next year the Future Teachers of America have a field." Pause. Will pretending to break a pencil in half. "Trip to New York City and the cost is twenty-seven

31

dollars. Fifty cents the following students report to guidance office immediately after final." Several people were sticking four fingers at their mouths to indicate that on the gag scale this was worse than usual. A four-finger gag is pretty serious. "Bell the school sweatshirts in the new designs are in the school store."

Everybody shuddered.

But not even Will breathed a syllable of correction. We were all awaiting Wendy's broadcast. We are addicted to Wendy's soap. It usually runs two minutes. This week we were worrying about whether Greg would change his socks and if Allegra was going to shave the right hemisphere of her skull and put a safety pin through her nose since she was dating a European rock star. There was also the problem Brandon and Octavia were having. Brandon seemed to be falling in love with Lulu.

Wendy has a very intense voice, as if somebody is holding a gun to her head while she reads.

"Brandon slouches against the tall brick column in the library. His eyes drift past Allegra, for whom he has nothing but scorn, and land longingly on Octavia. Octavia is being cruel to him. 'Brandon,' says Octavia, her lips curled, 'I want a real man, with a real name. Dirk, perhaps. Or Lance. Someone on his mission impossible, saving the nation from certain doom. And what are you, Brandon, but a well-dressed Yuppie on his way to his first million? Do I care whether you have a Gucci jockstrap? No. I cannot seem to—'"

And Wendy was off the air.

It had happened once before when Wendy had Brandon and Octavia shack up together. Dr. Schneider got quite fierce about that. I guess Dr. Schneider did not care to have Wendy mention jockstraps, even designer models, over the school P.A. system. Everybody in American history grinned, getting a kick out of the silence, to see if Wendy would come back on.

But she didn't. The next announcement was from a guidance counselor about the deadline for applying to something or other. I never listen to guidance counselors.

We all went racing out of class immediately, but me faster than the rest. Parker is allowed to drive one day a week, and this was the day. Parker tries hard to leave without me so he can be alone with Wendy. I sympathize with them, but I'd rather be a pain than take the bus. I guess my romantic ideals apply more to me than to others.

The crosswalks were jammed with parents in cars coming for their kids. As I stood in the crowd waiting, Wendy and Parker emerged hand in hand from the office complex, laughing. Whatever objection Dr. Schneider had to that episode, she'd won. Parker leaned down a little toward Wendy, and she stretched up, and their heads rested against each other.

The person next to me sighed.

Jeep.

Eyes fastened on my brother and Wendy. Handsome mouth turned down sadly. Head tilted wearily. He still wanted to be the shoulder on which Wendy rested.

Wendy never glanced our way. She was completely absorbed in Parker, and when they kissed, their intimacy quotient was as high as it gets. Jeep sighed again. And he didn't glance my way either. Whatever Wendy had, I didn't.

But what did I expect—me with my intimacy quotient of forty-seven, me in need of professional help because I couldn't relate to boys? Did I really think Jeep would suddenly spot me and forget all about Wendy, and want nothing but me?

I reached the car just as Park and Wendy did. Wendy

glared at me. Does his little sister have to show up right now? Couldn't she drop dead somewhere so we could have an hour alone? "I could drive," I said brightly. "Then you could have the backseat."

"Uh-uh." Parker was firm. "The backseat is your territory, kid. Always has been, always will be."

Kid. He was a whole ten months older.

He opened the front door for Wendy. I got in by myself. This is my life, I thought: alone in the backseat. I sighed heavily, but nobody heard. Parker and Wendy were having their pre–driving-out-of-the-parking-lot kiss.

Happily ever after, huh? On the great board game of Romance, I was still at square one.

3

♥ Interlocked hearts are hard.

They have dead ends. You can't get your players from one heart to the next. If you add little connectors, you get this jumble of left and right turns and you can't tell where to go.

My original attempt of six interlocked hearts turned into gridlock: more traffic jam than game.

My second design had the six hearts facing in a circle, points to the center, and little ribbons attaching them. You swung around the hearts and over the ribbon to the next heart. My hearts looked more like misshapen apples. Drawn by a kindergartner. A kindergartner with visual problems.

My third design was one enormous heart with four layers. You circled the heart first on the red path, then the rose path, then the pink, and finally the lavender. It was fun to color. I divided each path into one-inch squares, which I would label for action or dates or something.

I counted the squares. Sixty per path, for a total of two hundred forty squares. I had to think up two hundred forty romantic events? Even my mother and father, with all those years of romance behind them, hadn't managed anything like that. Most of their romance was repeat anyway: the usual flowers, dinner out, and Hallmark cards. But hey, that was three—only two hundred thirty-seven to go.

I did my sketching in the back of my history notebook.

Faith had to watch basketball practice. Now that Angie had had lunch with her, she figured she was a member of the team. The coach is pretty loose about kids sitting on the bleachers, as long as you're quiet. There's usually at least a dozen kids lounging around, half watching practice and half in a stupor from school.

We sat on the top so we could rest our backs against the wall. The poor boys—fourteen of them, including junior varsity—were being subjected to various forms of torture. Right now they were running like madmen toward the opposite gym wall, hurling themselves feet-first against it and using the leap to turn around and race back.

It's one thing to do that in a swimming pool: The water's going to catch you if you fall. You're not going to break your neck, twist your ankle, or crack your ribs. It was a good thing I had the Romance game to design. I could stop watching the boys playing suicide with their bones and concentrate on my hearts.

Kenny—he of megaloser fame—is a scorekeeper. He wanders in and out of all athletic things, on the fringes of them as he is on every other activity, and today after wandering over to the coaches, he wandered up to us. "Hello, Kenny," said Faith in a very unwelcoming voice.

Kenny smiled at her—Kenny, who might brush his teeth on a monthly basis and undoubtedly replaced his shirt for the very last time in seventh grade—and said, "Hi, Faith. Hi, Kell. What's new?"

I detest that question. You immediately start to wonder what *is* new in your life, and of course, *nothing* is new in your life, it's the same old routine. Or if there *is* something new, you certainly don't want to tell Kenny about it. Why didn't he just say "How're ya doin'?" like a normal person so you could say "Fine" and be done with it?

Of course, Faith did have something new and wonderful in her life: Angie. And she took a deep, happy breath because she was dying to tell somebody about it. But once her lungs were full, she remembered it hadn't happened yet, and something might go wrong, and did she really want to boast about it before the event? And then she looked at Kenny and realized she really would rather die than discuss anything with him, so she just let all the air out again and pretended to be excited about the boys' exercises.

Kenny is used to being left out of things, and he knew he was being left out of whatever Faith was going to say, so he looked at me for a response. I was flipping the pages in my spiral notebook to hide my heart sketches. Kenny's hand flew out and slid between the pages to flip back whatever I was hiding.

"Hearts," said Kenny slowly.

I would have ripped it away, but I didn't want to tear the pages.

"Hearts," he said again thoughtfully. "You've never come to basketball practice, Kelly. Today you come. Today you sit drawing your little hearts and trying to hide them. Today you changed seats so you'd be next to Will. Today you and Will talked." Kenny smiled joyously. "So that's it, huh? You're crazy in love with Will, aren't you?"

"I am *not*," I said. "I am just drawing *hearts*. I like hearts."

37

" 'Cause you're in love," agreed Kenny.

"I am not in love. These hearts have nothing to do with Will. I'm just . . . I'm—uh—just playing a game."

Kenny grinned. "That's what it is, kid. A game. But it's more fun with another player. How about I go clue Will up, in case he's too dense to catch on?"

"No!" I screamed. "Don't you dare!"

The coach looked up at us and glared.

The entire basketball team looked up at us and glared.

I shrank down into my seat, making little apology faces, and Kenny stood there laughing. "Guess I'll tell Will," he said, and trotted down the bleachers, across the gym floor, narrowly missing death by trampling, and sat on the bench next to the water jugs. Sooner or later Will would come for a sip of water.

"I'm going to die," I said to Faith.

Faith flipped the spirals open herself and frowned at my hearts. "Is Kenny right? Are you in love with Will?"

"No."

I wonder why we always deny love. I remember in junior high if you were accused of the crime of loving, you screamed denials constantly, and stopped ever even *looking* at the boy you were accused of liking. I remember how the boys could destroy each other by yodeling, "Toby loves Jen-nie," and both Toby and Jennie would cringe and blush.

I mean, love is this great thing that most songs and books and poems and lives are all about.

So the minute we actually think there might be love around, we start laughing and pretending and hiding from it.

I was hiding my hearts under the spirals.

If I really do fall in love one day, I thought, will I hide it? What happens if you hide love so well, the person you love thinks you don't care? How come you can't just walk up to somebody and say, "Gee, I love you."

Faith said, "Kenny just told Will. Look over there."

I made the mistake of looking over there. Will was bent over the water jug, drinking from the spout, which is not allowed, and, surprised by whatever Kenny had said, twisted midstream to stare our way. Water spewed onto the gym floor. Kenny tossed a towel over the spill. Will twisted back, pretzel-fashion, and straightened up. All this while staring at us.

Actually he must have been staring at *me*, but we were too far to see his eyes, and I felt safer thinking it was both of us drawing Will's attention.

Will waved at us.

"Wave back," hissed Faith. "Don't be such a *lump*, Kelly. Take *action*."

I waved back.

Will jogged onto the court to join the action again.

"I have to get out of here," I said.

"*Why?* He *waved* at you!"

"Faith, I don't even *like* Will."

"Then why are you drawing the hearts?"

"Faith!"

"Just teasing you," said Faith, leaning all over me like a cat wanting its chin scratched. "I think waving back is a good sign. I think it means there are possibilities here. I think it would be fun to have me date Angie and you date Will. We'd have two fifths of the basketball team sewed up."

"Good grief," I said

And I took the late bus home before practice ended. Before I had to think about dealing with Will.

♥

"Oh, George, you shouldn't have!" cried my mother, taking the tiny wrapped gift with delight. This time he'd brought a white lace bookmark, six inches long, an inch wide: thread spun into a row of hearts.

Nobody ever spun a row of hearts for me.

Members of the opposite sex, report to my house! Gift in hand. Kiss on lips.

"That's lovely, Mother," I said enthusiastically. I gave Daddy a hug. "You're such a sweetie," I told him. "I should be so lucky."

He shared hugs with Mother and me. "Your time will come, Kelly. I don't mind if it's slow arriving. I kind of like my baby girl."

I mind if it's slow arriving. Once when Parker was on the phone and he didn't know I could hear him, he called Wendy his baby girl. Oh, to have a boy call me that.

I wondered what Angie would call Faith.

"Let's go out to dinner," said Daddy, exclusively to Mother.

"Oh, George. I already started dinner. I've got the pot roast nearly done and the potatoes—"

"That's always better the second day. Come on. I'll call a restaurant. You want Chinese? French? What are you in the mood for?" This triggered Daddy's musical memory, and he began singing loudly "I'm in the Mood for Love." My father has a terrible voice and worse rhythm.

I was glad Parker wasn't home yet. He always ruins it by telling Daddy if he can't reach the notes, don't sing the song. Details, details.

Sometimes we go out as a family, but more often my parents go out alone. This is one of the things that Megan says is abnormal about the Williams family. She says once you have children, you are obligated to take them with you wherever you go. Especially if you're going to a nice restaurant. Megan says my parents are selfish. I say they're romantic, and Megan is just jealous.

Parker came bounding in, saw my mother looking for her heavy coat and said, "You're going out? But can I still take Mother's car? I'm going somewhere with Wendy."

"May I," corrected my mother, and "Where with Wendy?" said my father.

"May I," said Parker. And to my father: "Don't know."

My father looked steadily at my brother. Parker looked steadily back. They didn't take their eyes off each other. A contest I didn't understand and Mother didn't see, because she was humming around getting ready for *her* date. Whatever the contest was, Parker won. My father dropped his eyes, grinned at nothing, and said, "You have enough money, Son?"

"Could use more."

Daddy gave him some, folded, so I couldn't tell how much, and Park was gone. Daddy held Mother's coat for her. "You going to be all right alone, Kelly?"

"Sure." The last thing they wanted this evening was to worry about me.

Daddy touched the earrings he'd given my mother at some anniversary, tiny silver violets, and the silver necklace that was last year's Christmas gift. "You're beautiful, Vi," he said softly.

My mother lit up, the way she does for compliments, and for one moment, she really *was* beautiful.

They left hand in hand.

In the TV room I slid the rented movie into the VCR and went back to the kitchen to pop popcorn. Then

I settled in front of the screen to compose my sociology quizzes.

My first thought was to have a hundred words everybody would check off for romantic value. But when I finished (lace, calorie-counting, candlelight, wallpaper), it was obvious everybody would check off the same words I did, and nobody would learn a thing.

Next I tried categories.

FOODS	COLORS	CARS	HOBBIES	PLACES
chocolate	scarlet	station wagon	holding hands	McDonald's
cough drops	royal blue	Porsche	playing tennis	ski resort
carrot sticks	black	dune buggy	bowling	campgrounds
wedding cake	avocado	limousine	hitchhiking	Disney World

Colors might be interesting. Maybe more boys than girls thought black was romantic. But under foods nobody would check off cough drops and under hobbies nobody would put hitchhiking ahead of holding hands.

I munched popcorn and got butter on the paper.

Was Faith on the phone with Angie?

Were they arranging their date?

Would everything work out for them? Or would Faith report back that she was right about *F* names: people who wore them were doomed to a fat, frumpy life with no romance?

"That's it!" I cried. "A name game!"

I'd list names. Which is more romantic? Ethel or Rosemary? Laura or LouEllen? Starr or Stefanie?

By the time the movie was over, I had written two sociology tests.

Kelly Williams
Sociology Four, Miss Simms

Romance Quiz Assignment

In this quiz we will find out what words make boys think of romance and what words make girls think of romance. You may check no more than ten words on this list.

WORD	BOY	GIRL
chocolate		
kitten		
dancing		
violin		
smoking		
flowers		
whipped cream		
tennis		
city skyline		
fame		
black		
sunshine		
snuggling		
novels		
high heels		
rings		

WORD	BOY	GIRL
stockings		
sparkles		
music		
ruffles		
sharing Coke		
strapless		
boots		
drumbeats		
candlelight		
plaid		
eyeshadow		
laughter		
stars		
Porsche		
listening		
patchwork quilt		
Fourth of July		
lavender		
September		
dark eyes		
diamonds		
velvet		

WORD	BOY	GIRL
scent		
midnight-blue		
tennis		
beaches		
silver		
snow		

Kelly Williams
Sociology Four, Miss Simms
Romance Quiz Assignment, page 2

In this quiz we'll find out if certain names automatically make a person feel romantically disposed or turn people off.

Give each name a romantic rating by checking the column to the right.

NAME	VERY ROMANTIC	RATHER ROMANTIC	NOT VERY ROMANTIC	TOTALLY UNROMANTIC
Amanda				
Adam				
Barbara				
Neil				
Emily				
Michael				
Faith				

NAME	VERY ROMANTIC	RATHER ROMANTIC	NOT VERY ROMANTIC	TOTALLY UNROMANTIC
Mark				
Gwen				
Paul				
Heather				
Scott				
Esther				
Keith				
Ashley				
Glenn				
Julie				
Frank				
Rodney				
Christopher				
Jessica				
Laurie				
Cameron				
Rich				
Holly				
Nellie				
Patrick				
Rudy				

NAME	VERY ROMANTIC	RATHER ROMANTIC	NOT VERY ROMANTIC	TOTALLY UNROMANTIC
Ed				
Wanda				
Ted				
Sam				
Rodney				
Charlotte				
Sarah				

I went to bed laughing. For once I had had a day packed with romance. Of course, it wasn't real. It was all games. Other people were doing it while I was writing it. But it turned out that romance was fun even on paper.

Good night, world, I thought. I hope you're ready for me.

Because I'm about to leave square one.

4

❤ I cannot believe now that I actually turned in those quizzes.

You would think sixteen years of life would have taught me to avoid public humiliation.

But no.

I ran toward humiliation as if it were male and in love with me.

In sociology Faith's eyes were fastened on Angie.

Angie's, however, were fastened at some point on his desk, where he kept putting things he could stare at: first his pen, then his book, then a pocketknife. Next, four quarters he stacked and restacked, as if playing a single's shell game. His cheeks were slightly flushed, and against his olive skin the ruddy color was unexpected and beautiful.

I convinced myself—against a lot of previous evidence— that Angie was in love as much as Faith and too shy to glance at her under the stress of such powerful emotion.

"All right, class. Pass in your quizzes," piped Miss Simms.

Each of us handed the homework down the row to the person in front, who would stack them and hand them to the left. Fatal for me, because Honey sits two seats in front of me. She covered her quiz with mine, stared into my typing, and at the top of her lungs yelled, "Oh, my *God*! Listen to *this*!"

Everybody listened, figuring something good was coming.

"Guess what Kelly wrote her quiz about!" shrieked Honey, laughing so hard, she had to hit the desktop with her palm. "You'll never *believe* it!"

She turned in her seat, taking the opportunity to turn her emerald-green eyes (she has dyed contact lenses; last year her eyes were plain old hazel) on Jeep and Will and Angie.

"What?" said Jeep, leaning way over his desk.

The entire rest of the class leaned way over their desks too. Faith frowned at me, with no idea what was coming. We'd talked about Angie so long, I'd forgotten to show her my quizzes.

Naturally Honey adored having Jeep lean toward her. She leaned right back. "Romance," she said in a low sexy voice. "Kelly's got not one, but two tests for us to take to see if we're romantic." Honey actually pointed at me, a long thin mocking finger. Every eye in class followed the finger and stared at me.

"I don't think you took this assignment seriously, Kelly," said Miss Simms. "I will be distressed if you simply imitated something foolish out of *Cosmopolitan*."

"Oh, Kelly's serious," said Honey. "She takes romance *very* seriously." Honey smiled and paused—for drama. In her way she's as good as Wendy. "Kelly's always studying those of us who have it."

I couldn't even duck my head and let my hair waterfall

over my face. I had to sit there and laugh and pretend to join in the fun.

I would be very lucky if I kept from crying.

"That's kind of neat," said Jeep. "Let's take her romance quizzes. Miss Simms, read them out loud."

I could not look anywhere. Ahead of me was Honey's pointing finger. To my left was Will. To my right, Wendy. I had to pick a point out of space and fix my eyes as if it were God, or my guardian angel. *Please rescue me. Please don't let this be happening.*

"Actually these will be quite interesting," said Miss Simms, looking through my papers. "We find out whether boys and girls agree if certain words signal romance."

It was Will's reaction I dreaded most. Will, whom Kenny had told I was in love with, drawing hearts over—Will, knowing I was passing in a romance quiz?

Oh, *how* could I have done this!

"We've got the whole period left, Miss Simms," said Jeep in a pleasant, cooperative, A-student voice. "Why don't I just run down to the department office, run off twenty copies, and we'll all take the test right now?"

"Good idea," said another boy. "I'm in a real rush to know if I'm romantic or not."

"You're not," the boys assured him. "You're a loser."

"But you can take lessons from me if you want," Angie said.

"You? Listen, Ange, the girls never go out with you twice. It'd have to be a quick lesson."

"You mean *I* never go out with a girl twice," Angie corrected. "I've got very high standards."

I risked a glance to one side. But Faith wasn't upset at all. She was wreathed in smiles. She knew she met the high standards.

Jeep, grinning, simply got up and took the quiz from an unprotesting Miss Simms. In less than two minutes he was back, his usual speedy self, passing the papers out. He was already laughing. "Wait till you read this, guys," he warned everybody.

"Take this seriously now," cautioned Miss Simms.

Everybody laughed raucously.

I wondered if you could blush to death. Perhaps it would say that on my death certificate. *Overheating from blushing caused the central nervous system—*

"Because," said Miss Simms, and her squeaky voice suddenly dropped an octave into normalcy, "because to love and to be loved are the greatest joys on earth."

There was complete silence.

It was a truth. More than we'd ever learn in science or math or history.

But who can tolerate the truth? Especially in front of their friends?

People wrote their names on their quiz sheets. They began reading the directions. And laughter began to riffle over the room again.

"Whipped cream?" said Angie. *"Whipped cream,* Kelly?"

I'm going to live with my grandmother, I thought. I'll never set foot in Cummington again.

"Chocolate, kitten, dancing, violin," read Honey. "Does anybody think that Kell is just a little bit deprived?"

"Boots," read Kenny. "But I don't see my other romantic favorites on here, Kelly. Where is leather, and whips and—"

"Class!" shrieked Miss Simms in her tiny pitiful scream. Brief silence settled, but it was muffled laughter, not vanished laughter. At me. "You're just envious of Kelly," said Miss Simms. "She has sufficient character to attack the important parts of life. What you care about and dream about

51

and struggle toward. And here you're trying to embarrass Kelly, when it's all part of you too!"

For a minute, perhaps two minutes, I thought she had saved me. I was actually able to breath in completely without that jagged edge that is the start of tears. I was able to let go of my pencil a little and release the cramps forming in my hand.

And Will said, "Crap."

The single syllable was fierce and angry.

"Sparkles? Flowers? Porsche? None of that has anything to do with love. This is stupid, Kelly. Love is promises. Generosity. Forgiveness. Kindness. Love is important stuff." Will looked at me with contempt. "Every single thing you've listed is shallow crap."

I had no defense. He was probably right. It was shallow. I must be too. After all, I was the one whose intimacy quotient was forty-seven.

"Will," said Wendy, "Kelly didn't write a quiz on love. She wrote a quiz on romance. What's wrong with romance? Romance is a backdrop to love. Don't be so high and mighty. If you'd relax a little, you might have romance in your life, too, instead of sweat pants and broken sneaker laces."

I could not remember when Wendy had contributed in sociology.

Will said uncomfortably, "I guess I see what you mean."

"Of course, you do," said Wendy. "Romance is soft music and sleek cars. Holding hands and a pretty dress. Love is none of those. Love is an emotion, not objects. Not surroundings."

For a moment the class was caught up in Wendy's voice. We shared faraway looks, and the dream was almost visible. *Let me have love.*

But Honey said, "Funny. Parker's car isn't sleek. And

Jeep's was. I guess you and Jeep were all romance and no love, huh, Wendy?"

Jeep froze. He didn't blush and fade like me: He simply ceased to breathe or be there.

Half the class attacked Honey for Jeep's sake. Miss Simms had to yell for quiet, but quiet never came. Even when the final bell rang, we were still saying ugly things and taking sides and poking at each other.

What is this thing called love, I thought, that turned this dull group into such an emotional mob?

I got up last, wanting to see nobody, talk to nobody, be reminded of nobody. Wanting to be dead, actually, but there was an important test next period I couldn't skip.

Will held the door for me.

"Thank you," I mumbled, stumbling through it, hating him for being there.

"Romantic of me, wasn't it?" he said sarcastically. As if doing romantic things were bad. He faked a smile.

"You've got a smile like a German shepherd," I told him.

We stood a moment staring at each other. I was so drained, I could hardly raise my chin, and looking up at Will required considerable raising of the chin.

"But you," he said softly, "have the smile of a pixie."

5

❤ A pixie?

Now, what is a pixie?

I think of a feathery elf with button features fluttering on gauze wings among magic toadstools.

At home I stared at myself in the mirror. The day's blush had finally faded, and I could see my features again. I do have a perky nose and a small chin. Is a pixie smile a good thing? *Was* Will being sarcastic when he held the door for me, or did I just read that into his voice because I was so upset?

"Oh, I don't want to wonder!" I cried aloud. "I want something to *happen*!"

I sagged into a chair. In the next room Mother was making supper: heating up the pot roast we had never gotten to. My father was teasing her.

There is romance, I reminded myself. I'm a witness.

I began to cry.

And Parker came in.

That's the way it is with families and classrooms. No privacy. Always somebody watching.

"What's the matter?" he said instantly. He didn't come sit next to me or hug me. We aren't physically close, Parker and I. He stood in the door, though, and waited patiently for an answer.

I shrugged.

"Has to be something. Maybe I can help."

The last thing I would ever do would be to admit what had happened in sociology. My romance game with Will. My feelings about life in general. Especially to Park, who didn't know why Wendy liked him any more than the rest of us did. "I was thinking of Mother and Daddy," I lied. "How romantic they are. Did you see the little heart bookmark?"

"Romantic? Garbage. There's nothing romantic about that."

Now, *that* was the most interesting remark my brother had ever made, and the most unlikely. "Nothing romantic?" I repeated.

"He doesn't bring those presents for romance. Don't you know anything, Kelly? He's just spreading oil on the waters."

"What waters?"

"Of their marriage. It's such a dumb marriage. I'm never going to have a fake marriage like theirs."

I was outraged. "A fake?" I sputtered. "Mother and Daddy?"

"They've been married eighteen years and any fool can tell Dad adores Mother, but Mom's so insecure, he has to go through this endless charade of proving himself, week after week, year after year, gift after gift, bookmark after bookmark, flower after flower."

It's strange to try to think of your own mother as

insecure. Insecure belongs to kids. Mothers are supposed to be solid.

"And all because of Ellen, who could even be dead by now for all we know."

"Ellen?" I repeated. "Daddy's high school girlfriend?"

We'd heard all about Ellen. She shared eight years of Daddy's life. His first trip to Europe, his first plane ride, his first weekend in New York, his first time on the West Coast, all with Ellen. Right after college Ellen jilted Dad. Just up and said she didn't love him anymore, good-bye. Have you met somebody else? asked my father. No, replied Ellen, I just don't want to spend my life with you.

Dad was shattered for about a month, but then he met Mother, and the romance of the century began between them.

"What could *Ellen* have to do with anything?" I said crossly. If Parker was going to make up some cheap story about how Daddy was really having an affair with Ellen on the side, I would kill him.

"Dad and Mom got married when they'd known each other six weeks. Talk about falling in love on the rebound! Dad had been seeing Ellen for *years*. She was the first and only girl Dad ever dated. Dad worshiped Ellen. And less than three months later he's married? Think about it."

I thought about it. Bewildered, I said, "But Parker, Mother and Daddy fell in love at first sight."

Parker spoke to me slowly, with forced patience. "Kelly, Dad would have married Ellen in a heartbeat. Mother was his *second* choice. And only because she was there. All this time Mother has never felt sure that Dad really loves her."

"Ridiculous. He brings her presents every five minutes. She must have noticed by now."

"Okay, don't believe me. But there's no romance in those gifts, Kell. He just has to keep shoveling this junk at her in

56

order to keep her happy. She's a grown woman acting about fifteen. Wendy doesn't act like that," he finished contentedly. "I tell Wendy I love her, she believes me, and that's that."

I resented his making Wendy sound better than Mother.

"Wendy and I," Parker said loftily, "have an *honest* relationship. No pretenses, like Mother and Dad." He pranced off to his room, singing scraps of melody. Love songs to Wendy. I gathered up my quizzes. Lace, chocolate, laughter, candlelight, dancing . . . not romantic?

I rejected the whole idea.

Because if Mother and Daddy's romance was fake, then whose could be real?

Parker thought his with Wendy was real.

It had lasted three months.

But how long does love have to last to be real? If Daddy had loved Ellen for eight years and nothing came of it, then what *was* love anyhow?

♥

Somebody made five hundred copies of my romance quiz and passed them out in the halls the next day at school.

Public humiliation builds character, I told myself. I smiled when people teased. I agreed that *plaid* and *whipped cream* were pretty weird words on a romance quiz.

Parker pounced on me in the halls. Waving my quiz in his hand, he said furiously, "I cannot believe my own sister actually did this."

"It seemed reasonable at the time."

"Kelly. The whole school—"

"I know, I know, don't say it. Just stand next to me like a decent big brother."

"It'd be easier if you were a decent little sister. Do you know how people are laughing?"

"Yes, Park. I know."

He relented. Park hadn't been voted Nicest Boy for nothing. Putting an arm around me, he said softly, "Good luck, kid. I think it's going to be a long week for you."

But hey. By the end of the day teasing had tapered way off. By last period not more than ten or twenty people even mentioned the quiz.

I stole a look at Will.

He was not stealing one at me. He was listening to the American history teacher. How can anybody concentrate on the Last Frontier when there are important things happening, like the girl next to you being totally humiliated, needing a new compliment—one she can put on the shelf next to "You have the smile of a pixie"?

Wendy came on with her soap. I relaxed, thinking it would take some of the heat off me.

"It's been a long weekend for our beauteous Allegra," said Wendy softly. "Allegra"—Wendy's voice heightened— "Allegra has taken—" Wendy's voice became frenzied, as if Allegra had taken an overdose, or maybe a flight to Switzerland. "Allegra has taken a quiz on romance! Her score is forty-seven! She has failed miserably. The entire world knows now that Allegra is totally lacking in romantic appeal."

I stared at Will's back.

How could he have done that? How could he possibly have told Wendy about that?

"Taking to her bed," cried Wendy, "Allegra will eat nothing but Classic Spam. No whipped cream. No violins playing. In vain Greg pounds upon her front door."

Everybody giggled. Everybody whispered, "Eeeeuuuh, Kelly."

Wendy played sound effects: three bars of violins, knocking on doors.

I had sound effects of my own to endure: laughter coming from every classroom at Cummington High. Laughter at me. I put my head down on my arms and hid from my world. Which of them was worse: Will or Wendy? Bad enough that Will told. But my own brother's girlfriend using me like that? Turning me into material? Boy, was she ever paying me back for riding in the backseat when they wanted to be alone.

Will's back remained motionless: broad and—in annoying coincidence—plaid. A wool plaid shirt I would gladly have strangled him with.

"Greg is not a man to glance backward," Wendy continued. "Jumping into his *sleek* car, Greg takes to the road." Every time she used a word from my quiz, she emphasized it, and giggled slightly. *Sleek* car.

"As he cruises past her house the alluring Octavia, gowned in *ruffles* and *midnight-blue,* rushes out. Greg slams on the brakes. 'Octavia! Octavia! What is *your* romance quotient? Come, take a test ride with me.' "

Faith said, "I think this is the best dialogue she's done in weeks."

Everybody else said, "*Shhhhhh!*"

"But Octavia is beyond romance." Wendy's voice turned throaty, and she rasped, " 'Forget romance, Greg,' says Octavia. 'I happen to be pregnant.' "

There was no need to say "*Shhhhhh*" this time. Silence reigned from everybody being totally stunned.

" 'What I need is money and marriage.' "

I don't suppose our teen pregnancy rate is different from the rest of the nation, but here in Cummington we certainly don't *refer* to it. Teen sex, if indeed there *is* such a thing, occurs beyond the city limits. I know, because the P.T.A. told us so.

In her bright wrap-up voice Wendy continued, "Tune in tomorrow to find if romance can—"

The mike went off.

Nobody breathed.

When the mike came on again, Dr. Schneider read two more announcements in a decidedly shaken voice. The class burst into a discussion of Wendy's soap dialogue. But they had forgotten the mockery of my quiz. They could talk only about Octavia's pregnancy and Wendy's nerve.

Now Will turned around: now when everybody was too caught up speculating about Wendy's future to notice him. Not for Will public humiliation. He turned, held up his hand like a STOP sign, and said very fast, "I didn't do it."

I curled my lip at him.

"Really. I didn't tell her. Honest."

"Oh, right. Wendy overheard us from the principal's office, huh? Two floors and a half mile of hall away."

"I don't blame you for suspecting me," said Will. "Any detective would. But I'm innocent. It's coincidence. She picked 47 out of thin air."

"No air," I informed him icily, "is that thin."

I truly felt like killing him. At least all that anger kept me from crying.

Will didn't give up. He was long enough to lean across the space between our desks, put both enormous hands on my books and look mournfully into my face. I considered smacking him but it would just draw more attention my way.

But he wasn't being a pain. He was truly upset. I looked into the conceited eyes that had never bothered to focus on me, and I realized that Will Reed really wanted me to believe him. He cared about my opinion of him.

I couldn't understand it. He *had* told Wendy, he could only have done it to be mean, so why care about me now?

"Could she have found your magazine?" said Will. "Maybe you left it out and she and Park found it, with your answers written in."

I meant to snarl at him, but I didn't get far. I had left the magazine in Park's car. Maybe she and Parker had taken the quiz. I had, like the stupid jerk I am, circled my answers. Wendy could add. Wendy would *love* adding that. Wendy Newcombe, Queen of Romance.

And a user.

I sighed, and nodded. "Could be, Will. Okay. I believe you."

Will's anxiety faded. He smiled into my eyes.

A real smile.

A boy's smile.

For a moment as long as crushes, our eyes locked. My heart was pounding. I struggled to say or do something, anything, that would keep him looking at me like that. (Invite him to make fudge? Throw a Frisbee? Ask him to show me his baby pictures?) But Will unfolded himself, stood up six feet four inches, and loped silently out of the room.

♥

At home there was trauma waiting.

My mother's trauma.

She was holding a letter in her hand, staring at it like a bomb. "What's wrong, Mother?" I said, instantly frantic, thinking death, dismemberment, fatal disease, the relatives in Ohio. . . .

"Your father's high school reunion," said my mother bleakly. "He wants to go. He can't *wait* to go. I have to send in our acceptance."

"Oh, but, Mother! That'll be such fun. Even I can't wait for my high school reunions. To find out what happened to

61

everybody? Whether they got what they wanted? If the Most Likely to Succeed really did? If we had any millionaires or famous movie stars or brilliant inventors in our graduating class? Ooooooh, Mother, you'll have a great time!"

My mother flopped onto the couch and drooped all over the pillows.

"No, huh?" I said. "Why not?"

She shrugged, getting even looser and more depressed all over the couch. My brother's dumb lecture on Mother and Daddy's marriage came back to me. "Because of Ellen?" I said dubiously.

She leaped to her feet. "Kelly, what made you think of Ellen? Does Daddy talk about her? Why did you think of Ellen first? How do you even know about Ellen? What is there to know?"

She was white. She ran her tongue over her lips and I thought, She is afraid of Ellen. Park was right.

"Because Daddy talks about her now and then, when he's telling stories about when he was young," I said, trying to be casual. "That's all."

Mother shivered and sat down again.

"Oh, Mother. Ellen's probably fat and repulsive. Has five kids who are all delinquents. Thinks a big day is making instant chocolate pudding."

"No, she isn't like that." An involuntary shudder rippled over her body and face. "Ellen already got her reunion invitation. She wrote to your father. She enclosed a photograph. She wants us to get together before the reunion."

"So what's she like in the photo? Can I see it?"

My mother's smile was forced. "She's beautiful. Looks ten years younger than she is. And you can't see it. Your father has the letter and photograph with him."

"With him? You don't mean in his wallet?"

62

"Maybe not in his wallet, but it's with him."

I sat down next to her, and for the first time in my life she leaned on me. "I know how silly this is," she said. I felt like a woman friend, someone on her side, not her little girl. It felt wonderful, even though she was scaring me. "Ellen is stunning. She always was. And he was excited to hear from her."

"Do you have the letter memorized? Quote it to me. I want to know what we're up against."

"Up against?" repeated my mother. "Kelly, I've felt up against Ellen for a long time. If I gain five pounds, I know Ellen would never lose her figure. If I forget the punch line to a joke I'm telling at a party, I know Ellen would tell more sophisticated jokes and never forget the ending. If I get all lazy for a few weeks, I know Ellen has unending energy, and everything she does is brilliant."

"Oh, I feel that way about half my class in school," I said, trying to joke.

And the doors were flung open, and in came Wendy and Parker. Mother ceased to be a woman with a woman and became a mother after school, offering Oreo cookies and ginger ale while the children chattered.

"So you got suspended for two days," said Parker to Wendy. "So it's not the end of the world."

"It *is* the end. I don't like to be in trouble. I just like to make a splash."

At my expense, I thought. I stared at Wendy, willing her to look sorry and guilty the way Will had, but she didn't notice me. It was so easy for her to use people she could forget in the space of a few hours.

Queen of Romance, I thought.

I was still envious of Wendy. I would *always* be envious of Wendy. But I no longer wanted to be Wendy.

Maybe she subconsciously wants Park's niceness to rub off on her, I thought. Maybe she's attracted to the one thing she doesn't have.

Wendy split her Oreos, licked the icing off, and set the uneaten chocolate halves back on the table. Nobody yelled at her. They thought it was cute. If *I* had done it, I would have been wasting expensive food.

Parker told Mother about the soap-opera dialogue, and how Dr. Schneider felt suspension was the only answer to Wendy's bad, bad thoughts. I thought death would be better, but I restrained myself from saying so. Then I would have to admit to my mother that I was the one with the forty-seven intimacy quotient.

"Well," said my mother, "the school doesn't like you to pretend that pregnancy can happen to juniors in high school."

For once Parker, Wendy, and I were utterly united. *"Pretend?"* we repeated.

Mother shuddered. "I prefer to believe that."

"You're wrong. You're an ostrich with your head in the sand," Parker said.

"I *like* being an ostrich with my head in the sand. I don't want details. Avoid details," she told us. She ate an Oreo cookie to distract herself.

"A good parent these days is supposed to be on the watch for clues that her children—"

"Hush. Now, Wendy, call your mother so she won't think you're running away from this."

"'Look who's talking," said Parker. "You're the one running away, Mom."

She ignored him and dialed Wendy's home number for her, handing over the phone. There's one thing Mother can't run away from, I thought. And that's Daddy's reunion and Ellen being there.

It seemed that Wendy's mother had already heard from Dr. Schneider. Dr. Schneider was certainly regretting that call. Mrs. Newcombe gave him a sharp lecture on civil liberties, the right to freedom of speech, the use of school airways, and the pregnancy rate at Cummington High.

Dr. Schneider decided he had been a little hasty giving a suspension to Wendy and of course he no longer meant it and yes Wendy could go on the air again tomorrow. Although he did insist that Octavia's pregnancy had to end.

Parker had several suggestions for how Wendy could end Octavia's pregnancy. Mother made him stop. Wendy said, "You know, you are kind of an ostrich with your head in the sand, Mrs. Williams."

"Go eat your Oreos," said my mother, and they left the kitchen.

I waited to see if Mother would bring Ellen up again, but she got out a cake mix and the bowls and beaters. I love cake mixes. No effort and minutes later you have a bowl to lick. I think it's too bad you even have to bake the cake. I like to eat the batter raw. Once I had a whole cup of batter.

She then put it all away without making anything. "No more desserts," she mumbled. "Have to lose ten pounds."

"Why?"

"This reunion. I have to look good at this reunion."

I would have laughed, except she was serious.

"You should have seen how your father put that photograph into his wallet," she said, leaning on the counter, as if the shelf for the mixer was too high, far too high, ever to reach again. "He slid it in like gold. Like precious—" she broke off.

And our conversation didn't continue. Mother fled to her room, something I do constantly but I had never seen her do.

I went to my room and opened my romance game board.

I wanted to be on the Start Heart with Will.

I wanted Mother and Daddy to be everlastingly at Happily Ever After.

I wanted—

"Kelly! Telephone!" shouted Park. He was irked. I understood. All phone calls should always be for yourself. No fair running to get the phone and it's for somebody else.

"Hello?" I said, wondering how much of this I felt like discussing with Faith.

"Kelly?"

It was Will. I recognized his voice instantly, just from my name. Will calling me up. I had to lie down.

"Hi, Will. How are you?"

"Wow. You knew my voice."

"Because you and I talk so much, you know. Disrupting every class."

Will laughed. He knew we'd had about two exchanges during our entire lifetimes. "Well, I guess Wendy rescued you," he said. "She didn't mean to, but everybody's already forgotten your romance quizzes, and they're talking exclusively about Octavia being pregnant and Wendy getting suspended."

"You make Octavia sound as real as Wendy," I told him.

"She is real. We all know more about what Octavia's doing than our own families. I was wondering if you're going to kill Wendy or not."

"I considered it. But Parker probably wouldn't like it."

"Why does he go out with her anyway?" said Will distastefully.

I was so struck by that. Everybody else wondered why

Wendy went out with Parker. Will couldn't understand why Parker went out with Wendy.

"I thought I'd tell you my intimacy quotient," said Will.

"I've been worried," I admitted. "Did you pass me? Are you capable of tons of intimacy or do you need counseling?"

"I got ninety-three. My social life is what everybody else aspires to."

"Maybe *you* should go out with Wendy," I said. "You could stack your conceit next to hers any day."

Will laughed. "Actually I made that up. The quiz was so dumb, I didn't bother to answer any of the questions. How can you stand stuff like that? It doesn't have anything to do with real-life romance."

But I don't *have* any real-life romance, I thought. I have to make do with whatever the magazines offer.

I turned the phone over in my hands a few times to untangle the cord. Ask me out, Will. Give me a real-life romance so I don't have to renew my magazine subscriptions.

"Actually," said Will very casually, "I have to go to this dinner dance. You knew I'm an All-State player, didn't you? No games, but an honor dinner and I have to go."

A few weeks ago I had disliked Will. I stared down at my lap at my board game, still open. My handsome boys, all nines and tens on a scale of attractiveness. There was Will, covering up Oriental Avenue. The game has to have sixes and threes and zeroes too, I thought. It should really be like sociology class: the stars, the losers, the medium, and the indifferent.

I jerked my mind off the stupid game. I was out of the game league. I was into the real thing. My first date with anybody at all on earth would be an important dinner dance with Will. I clung to the phone, waiting.

"And what I want to ask is," said Will, taking an exceptionally deep breath, "I know Megan's a really good friend of yours, and I don't know if she's still going out with Jimmy or not, so I thought I'd ask if you know what her situation is."

It truly felt as if the ceiling had lowered. It was pressing me into the ribcord, laughing at me, squashing my hopes, my pride, and my body. Oh, was life ever a game. And such fun too.

"They've split for good," I said smoothly, as if it didn't hurt.

"Oh."

So what happened to the pixie smile? I thought. Is Megan's pixier? Or is *pixie* an insult, not a compliment?

"So why'd you bring up the Romance Quiz, Will?" I said. "You want my opinion on what's romantic for this dinner with Megan?"

That embarrassed him. We finished the conversation sniping at each other—the kind of conversation I'm sure Honey always has: half nasty. I hated it. I wanted to say sweet things, good things. But Will wanted to say them to Megan.

At last he managed a good-bye.

To keep from crying I sketched board game cartoons.

Jimmy walking the squares with Megan. Jimmy gaining a bowling partner. Jimmy tossing Megan to the sidelines. Will rolling a double and heading for Megan. Faith rushing headlong through the curves. Parker and Wendy three squares away from Happily Ever After. Jeep losing turn after turn.

Suppose you were dealt a hand. Suppose you had a deck of fifty-two boys. Suppose some were great and some were mixed, and some made you throw up.

LANCE	BART	JOEL	KEVIN
tall	shrimp	fat	lean
rich	millionaire	beer drinker	mountain climber
lazy	good dancer	drives a bus	sexy
funny	stingy	generous	cute

Okay, you deal out the cards. Then what would you do with them? Trade them with other players? Run into roadblocks where you had to surrender one and gain another? Have a card of your own where you had to impress the boy cards so they'd stay with you?

How awful.

Too much like life.

I wanted the romance game to be fun, and I wanted always to come out a winner. Why play a game if you're going to be a loser?

I stared at the game half the night because it was better than weeping over Will. Actually I wouldn't have wept over Will because I still didn't really like him. I would have wept over me, because nobody loved me.

Around midnight Parker came in.

Since we had school the next day, he was in serious trouble. I knew Daddy was waiting up for him. I braced for the shouting. But there was none. Quiet talking at the foot of the stairs. And then Daddy's voice, quiet as a pat. "Okay, Son. Try to get some sleep. It'll be better in the morning."

Better in the morning? A car accident maybe?

"Oh, right," said Parker sarcastically. He came heavily up the stairs. I pretended to be going to the bathroom for a glass of water. "Wow, Park," I said. "What were you and Wendy up to? Midnight on a school night?"

My brother stopped in the narrow hall.

His light Windbreaker rubbed against the wallpaper with a slick, whispery sound. The night-light from the plug near our knees gave a shadowy cast to his features. His eyes were pools of dark, and his hair seemed longer, his shoulders wider, in the half dark.

When he spoke, his voice was like lead.

"We split. Wendy went back to Jeep."

6

♥ Where is the fun in a game that leaves one of the players absolutely devastated?

Wendy, presumably, was off having a wonderful time with Jeep. And Jeep, who had wanted her so much, was undoubtedly having a wonderful time with Wendy.

But Parker could not eat, would not speak, did not concentrate, and stayed off the phone.

Mother made Park his favorite meals. Daddy volunteered to go places with Parker that usually he claimed he was too tired to take Park to—like the ice hockey games at the Coliseum.

Parker simply ignored them, or glanced briefly in their direction as if they were crazy.

Perhaps they were.

Whatever Parker had felt for Wendy, it was far too deep to be assuaged by a pair of tickets to a hockey game. I could actually see Parker ache. Seventeen, and his joints were stiff and he moved slowly and unwillingly. When the phone rang, he'd stiffen and look at the phone as if it were the enemy, but with the potential of being his closest friend. His Wendy.

But Wendy never called.

Did Wendy ever love him? I wondered. What *is* love anyhow?

How can Parker have had so much of it and now it's simply gone? Is love an electric current? Throw a switch, and now it flows elsewhere? While the other love vanishes like a burned-out light bulb?

My own thoughts were filled with Will. I have never thought about a boy so intensely. I still didn't really like him. What had he ever done that was appealing, or friendly, or kind—or any of those things he himself listed under love?

I knew what a crush was from Faith's endless descriptions, and I had a crush on Will. Why? I thought despairingly. Why on the boy who actually calls me up to discuss another girl with him?

Angie didn't ask Faith out either.

Faith should have known. And I think she did know. It was just too unbearable to contemplate: being rejected. Both she and Parker were walking wounded. Parker bled internally and never talked. But Faith talked. Endlessly. I never told her about Will. There was nothing to tell. And yet the emotions were incredibly strong, and totally private.

In sociology Wendy was her usual bubbly self.

"How could she go out with Park three months," I whispered to Faith one class, "and it doesn't show? Nothing left of it?"

"It's as if they wrote that love in the sand at low tide," said Faith romantically, "and the waves wiped it away. There's no record left."

Wendy continued to write her soap operas. They continued to be funny. Whatever happened to Octavia's pregnancy we never learned over the loudspeaker system. School jokes about possible endings to that were told for days. Wendy thrived on the attention. She wrote her dialogue exclusively during sociology now, passing the scripts over to Jeep for his approval. Jeep invariably told her today's soap was the best ever.

At home the game of romance included history.

"For God's sake, Violet!" shouted my father one night at dinner. "It's nothing but a meal. Three hundred people having overcooked roast beef and telling each other we don't look any different. That's all the reunion will be."

"I understand, George. I understand perfectly."

"Good. Ellen is in the past, that's all. We'll have this one dinner with her and her husband what's-his-name, and that's it."

My mother stared into her water glass and whirled it until the ice cubes tinkled against each other.

"Ellen was always a very kind and understanding person," said my father.

"Oh? Am I going to require extra kindness and understanding?" said my mother furiously.

"Violet! Ellen will be an excellent hostess. You'll love her."

"You mean, *you'll* love her."

"I do not love Ellen."

"Then why do you keep bringing her up?"

A week of dinner-table conversations like that, and we were all ready to shoot somebody. It was just that we couldn't agree who deserved to be shot.

Ellen for existing?

Mother for overreacting?

Daddy for losing his temper and stomping off?

73

One night Parker said to me, "See what I meant? See how ridiculous this all is? Mom is weak and Dad is dumb."

"That's not true," I said, although it appeared to be.

"I don't know what Mom thinks is going to happen," muttered Park. "Does she think old Ellen is going to snatch Dad away from her? That Ellen will divorce what's-his-name and Dad will divorce Mom?"

It terrified me. "I suppose that could happen." If it did, I would definitely find that counselor. Forget my intimacy quotient. I would never survive my parents' divorce.

"It could not happen," said Parker sharply.

"You had faith in Wendy, and look what happened when the competition showed up."

Parker didn't argue. He just faded. The lines in his face deepened until he could have been Dad's age.

"What happened anyway?" I said. I hated not knowing. Not only did it mean I couldn't answer when the entire school asked me about Park and Wendy, it meant I couldn't help Park either.

My brother's answer, when it came, was the last I could ever have expected.

"I yelled at her for mocking you," he told me.

"But—but you were all worried about her when we sat in the kitchen with Mom," I protested. "You didn't say one word about her using me then."

"I didn't know then. She told me when we went out that night. About finding your quiz in the magazine, and figuring out your score, and deciding to use it."

"You defended me?" I said slowly. I thought: His love life ended because he was his usual nice self—about his dumb little sister who's always a pain when he has the car?

"She picked a fight. It was like she wanted a fight so she could stomp off and go back to Jeep. I felt like we were

74

following one of her scripts. She was laughing at you. She said you were a—" Parker stopped, didn't say whatever word Wendy had used, and went on. "And I got furious and yelled at her, which I have never done before, and she started whacking me with her purse and demanding a dime so she could use the pay phone and call Jeep to rescue her."

I couldn't even picture it. How absolutely horrible for Park! To have to sit there in his car while Wendy changed drivers! To have Jeep demand why did Wendy need rescue? Was Park hurting her? Was Park a monster?

We were sitting on my bed. Park slumped against the headboard.

"Oh, Park," I said, heartsick for him. "You'll find somebody else," I said cheerily. "Don't worry too much."

What a jerk I sounded like.

What a jerk I *am,* I thought.

I loved my brother for standing up for me, and yet if this was the result, he should have laughed with her. But he was nice. He wouldn't laugh at anybody, even me.

"I don't want somebody else." Despair in his voice matched the lines on his face. It's better to have played the game and lost, I thought, than to be like me, never playing at all. Nobody's voice ever sank in despair because of me, and I never felt despair because of them either. At least Parker can feel pain.

I tried to explain that.

"Kelly, it's like telling a cancer victim now that he's dying, he can appreciate life. It's stupid. I don't want to be a better, stronger person because of this. I want to be plain old me with Wendy at my side."

♥

By now my board game was a huge heart with three paths: one scarlet, one dusty rose, and one pale pink. You went around the heart three times and ended up in the center, resting on Cupid's arrow. Little cherubs danced around, and wedding bouquets fell into your final square. I'd spent hours cutting little illustrations from old magazines—February was the best issue—and gluing them on because my drawing was lousy.

I had divided the paths into squares. Each was a Good Thing. Nice dates, sunny weather, sleek cars, lovely gifts, hugs and kisses. I'd had such fun making up those dates. Never wrote so many exclamation marks in my life.

A picnic by the sea! Sunburned but happy!

A drive in a midnight-blue Porsche! Windblown and in love!

You two go hang-gliding and survive! Take another turn!

That night my brother was devastated, my mother terrified, my father irritable, and me lonely.

How dumb the game was. In real life nobody deals you a perfect anything, let alone rows of boyfriends. And spend every day, every square, doing something perfect with this perfect person?

I kicked the board game under my bed so Parker wouldn't see it.

7

♥ "No," said Megan. "Absolutely not, Mrs. Williams. It is wrong, wrong, wrong, wrong, wrong."

My mother looked longingly into my full-length mirror.

"You have become invisible," Megan told her. "You are wearing a skin-tone dress. Flesh colored makeup. Clear nail polish. I forbid you to wear this to the reunion."

"I kind of like being invisible," said my mother.

"Then you're a success," Megan told her. "People won't be able to shake hands with you because they won't be able to *find* your hand against that dress."

She definitely was no match for anyone in that outfit. It was queer how I too had come to think of Ellen as competition to be fought down. I wanted my mother to win. Easily. We ought to have *one* winner in the family at least.

"Go put on the purple dress," Megan said firmly. "Really. We're not kidding. It's perfect. The saleswoman who talked you into buying it had perfect taste. Put it on, and then we'll accessorize you." Megan turned to me. "God knows, after all the years of gifts from your father, she must have more accessories than the department store anyhow."

"But not many that go with purple," said my mother, trying to delay the moment of actually putting on the dress.

"Yes, you do," I told her. "You have at least a billion violet things."

"Violet is not purple. Violet is sweet, dark lavender. That dress I just spent a small fortune on is as purple as strobe lights." Mother heaved a huge deep aging sigh and slunk back to her room to try it on.

"I had no idea high school reunions were so scary," Megan said to me. "Especially when it's not even her reunion."

I did not see fit to explain Fear of Ellen and how it ranked in our family. I did not want the problem to become Fox Meadow property. "Mother just feels she's going to be on display, and she's a little nervous. Now, go back to telling me about Will. You actually turned him down?"

Megan contrived to look content and plump and house-wifely. "Yes. I loved turning him down. I felt so good afterward."

I lay on my bed. In the next room I could hear Mother rustling, slithering out of one dress into the next. I could feel the hard ribs of the pink spread digging into my bare skin. I could feel myself inside my clothes. But I could not feel what Megan was feeling.

"It's power," explained Megan. "Jimmy had such power over me. He could ruin my schedule, reduce me to tears, leave me feeling foolish and ugly and unloved."

"But that was Jimmy. This was Will."

"You don't understand," said Megan, which was certainly true. "Jimmy likes that drippy little bowling freak better. Did you see her? A loser. It's worse losing out to a loser than to a winner." Megan made a series of terrible faces which she admired in my mirror.

I wondered if that was how Ellen felt. Did she now think she was wrong to leave Daddy? Did Ellen think that Mother was a loser? Did she wonder how Daddy could choose Mother after her—beautiful, brilliant Ellen?

"I've never been dumped before," confided Megan. "And I never want to be dumped again. I'll always be the dumper, not the dumpee."

"You mean," I said slowly, "you said no to Will because it made you feel better about Jimmy?"

Megan smiled and nodded. "Ooooh, what great nail polish," she cried, landing on the gift boxes Faith was always raiding. "I saw this advertised in *Seventeen*. Can I try it, Kell? Thanks." She picked up the polish, unscrewed the top, glanced toward the door and shouted, "No, no, Mrs. Williams, that's even *worse*."

My mother shrank in.

"That color," said Megan, "is vomit-green. That's the dress old widow women wear when they're weeding in their gardens. You may *not* have it on your body. In fact, I don't think you should have it in your house."

Inside my clothes I was thin. My skin felt all silky from a shower and then perfumed talc. It was weird to lie there, so aware of myself physically, as a girl, and yet all the attention was on Megan or my mother, not me. Nobody else knew my body existed.

"Anyway, it makes you look fat," said Megan. "Other people at the reunion will be thin."

My mother cringed.

"They'll lord it over you if you look fat," said Megan, ramming the point home.

"I'm dieting," said my mother desperately. "I really am. I'm down two pounds."

Poor Will. He had no importance to Megan at all. She didn't even turn him down because of *him;* he wasn't worth turning down even. She turned him down because of Jimmy. And he would never know. He would wonder if it was his breath, or his personality, or his bony face, or smelly feet. (Actually I didn't know if his feet smelled. I had never had the opportunity, if that's what you call it, to find out; it was just an example.)

Megan was more interested in trying out my nail polish than in Will.

"And two pounds is wonderful," said Megan quickly. "I admire you for it. Now show us the purple outfit."

If there is a God, I thought, He could make Ellen gain weight between now and the reunion. Develop a craving for cream-filled doughnuts so she has to show up in size forty-four polyester pants.

But Ellen was the kind who would never get fat. I knew that from her yearbook picture. She would always manage to be superior to the others. Like Megan.

Megan was helping over Mother's clothes, but she wasn't really doing it to be helpful. She was showing Mother that she, at sixteen, knew more about style than Mother ever would. She was lording it over Mother and enjoying every minute.

Do I even like Megan? I thought. She's my lifelong friend, and now I don't think I like her. I don't like how she treated Will, and I don't like how she's treating Mother.

I thought how Daddy was treating Mother. He had stopped bringing presents and cards. I thought he was simply annoyed with her behavior. Mother thought it proof he was dreaming of Ellen.

Over Ellen they were going to break down.

Ellen, who lived two thousand miles away.

What terrible timing it all was.

Perhaps what my board game needed was an element of timing. Good timing and bad. Things that came together by accident as well as by planning. Things that would fall apart when nobody wanted them to, and things that would never have an explanation.

Mother came in wearing the purple dress.

"Oooooh!" screamed Megan, clapping. "It's *you*. Streamlined and feminine at the same time. I love how that fabric falls. And it's your color. Definitely."

I liked Megan again. My mother was smiling. Nervously. But smiling.

"You'll make a real splash, Mother," I told her. "I love it."

Mother looked hopeful.

"All you need now," said Megan authoritatively, "is one really good necklace. Something that makes a statement."

Mother looked helpless.

"That enormous silver violet on the silver rope that Daddy gave you years ago," I suggested. "The one you thought was too big to wear, remember? And you let me wear it one Halloween when I was a gypsy."

My mother made a face. "It's repulsively big."

"Not with this dress. It'll be perfect."

"I think I've hidden it too well ever to find it again," said my mother, perking up.

"Forget it, Mother. I know where it is." I raced to my parents' bedroom. All Fox Meadow houses have walk-in closets: two per master bedroom. Mother's flows over into Daddy's, and she keeps the presents she doesn't know what to do with in gift boxes tucked in odd corners. Megan went with me. She loves to snoop. "When's the reunion?" she wanted to know. "Tonight? Tomorrow?"

"Of course not. It's a whole month away. In this household we leave lots of time to panic in."

I unearthed a vast silver violet.

"Ouch. She's right," said Megan.

We went back and draped it around Mother's neck anyhow. "It *is* large," admitted Megan. She smiled brilliantly. "But the *effect* is *awesome*. Wear it. Well, I have to run. Places to go, boys to see." She smiled even more brilliantly and raced out of the room, narrowly missing Parker coming up. The house was like a thoroughfare.

"I wish I had someplace to go that made me so happy," said Parker, glancing after Megan. "Listen, Mom, do we have anything good to eat in this house?"

"Yes. And if you'll eat every bite of it, then I won't. Deal?"

Parker laughed. "Deal."

They went companionably downstairs. I went back to my own room and fished the board game and crunched-up boy cards out of my garbage. Luckily emptying garbage is my job, and I so rarely do it that I don't have to worry about losing anything. Nothing was wrinkled beyond repair. I got out my iron and ironed it. Then I began erasing every fourth or fifth good thing on the board and sticking in terrible, painful, agonizing, inexplicable stuff instead. They were much easier to think up than good things.

I erased *Sunshine*.

I put in: *He never calls; you never know why. Lose one turn*.

I erased a *Delirium of Love* square. I wrote *Abandonment*.

I got rid of *Crazy with Happiness* and tossed in *Depression*.

Then I replaced *Depression* with *Melancholia*. That sounded *really* depressed.

The phone rang.

I picked it up absently.

"Hi, Kelly. It's Will."

If I was surprised the first time, I was astounded the second. "Hi, Will."

"You do your sociology yet?"

"I breezed through the chapter. It was English that killed me. William Faulkner. I haven't understood a single sentence since page one, but somehow I've arrived at page seventy-three anyhow."

Seventy-three! I thought. That was my stable-marriage score. I wonder what this means. It's got to be significant.

"That's a lot to plow through," said Will. "We've been spared Faulkner in our class." He began telling me about things he didn't understand a word of either: a law in physics and a rule in basketball.

"And Megan turning you down?" I said before I could think.

Oh, what's the matter with tongues? Why aren't they latched to minds? Now he'd know that we'd gossiped about it. That Megan joyfully told everybody.

Into the silent phone I babbled, "It was mean of her, but it didn't have anything to do with you. It was Jimmy. She's still mad at Jimmy. It made her feel good to take it out on a boy. Any boy."

The silence continued.

I had run out of babble.

Will said, "I think you are the first girl I've ever run into who honestly says things. Truth, and all that. You're remarkable, Kelly."

Forget remarkable, I thought. Tell me sexy and beautiful.

We began talking. For almost an hour we talked. We covered girls, dates, Megan, Jimmy, truth, lies, Miss Simms, and Wendy's soap. I loved it. I could have talked all night to

Will. The more he talked, the more I liked him. The less conceited he sounded.

The more my crush came back.

Do I want this? I thought.

Do I have any choice? I thought five minutes later.

"Got to get off the phone," said Will cheerfully. "My father is glaring at me. I'm half an hour over my time limit."

"Oh," I said. "I'm sorry. I—I had more to say."

Will laughed. "Me too. See you tomorrow, Kell. Thanks for listening."

And he was gone.

I walked into the bathroom to look at myself in strong light, and see if there was a girl there that Will Reed could have a crush on.

There were two ways to read "See you tomorrow, Kell."

One: We share fourth and sixth periods, and at some point his eyes will naturally focus in my direction.

Two: He can hardly wait for tomorrow to come so he can see me. Kelly Williams. Good listener.

Actually I wasn't sure I liked that closing line. "Thanks for listening." That sounded very sisterly. Very "good friends." I hate friends. I want dates.

I wandered back into my room.

Parker was lying on my bed, holding my board game up over his head, reading the squares and laughing like a maniac.

"You scum!" I shrieked. "You rotten, worthless brother! You spy! Get off my bed. Stop reading that. Stop laughing at that. That's private, Parker Williams. I hate you!"

Parker merely swung the game out of my reach and kept laughing. "Kell, this game is terrific. It's so funny. I love it."

I had not meant anything to be funny. I wanted it to show the sweet side and the bleak side of romance.

"But Kell," he said, sitting up, crossing his ankles and spreading the game before him the way I always did, "you've designed it so only girls can play. Revise it all. Make it so boys can play too. Girl cards, and girl pronouns, and girl names as well as boys."

"How can I do that? That's too hard."

He patted my bedspread beside him so I'd sit there. Parker and I so rarely do things together that I was honored. Even if it was my own bed and my own game, it was nice to be asked.

"All the sentences are like *He loves you* or *He brings you flowers*. Change those. Make it *Your date loves you*. Or *Your date brings you flowers*. That way the date can be a boy or a girl."

I thought about that. It wouldn't be too hard to do. Just a lot of erasing. Pretty soon I would have erased right through the paper. It probably wouldn't kill me to start the game on fresh poster board, I thought.

Parker kept reading. *"He takes you to Europe. He brings you a dozen red roses. He teaches you how to water-ski."* Parker lowered his head like a Neanderthal man and stuck his jaw in my face. "You know, you're pretty sexist, Kelly. You're making the guy do everything."

"No, I'm not sexist. This is *my* game. For *me*. I can't put *She brings you a dozen red roses*. That's sick. And you can't write *He or she brings you a dozen red roses*. That's stupid."

"Right. You put *Your date brings you*." Parker began erasing. He was a very careful eraser. As he erased I rewrote. It was a kind of nice team.

"Furthermore," said Parker, "exactly how old and how rich are these dates of yours? Instead of skiing in Switzerland and a cruise in the Caribbean, you should share French fries at McDonald's and go bowling at Alley Nine. Real stuff."

Now he got into erasing with a vengeance. Eraser specks flew across the bedspread. Park took out the really good ones (scuba diving in Bermuda) and stuck in *You work at a car wash together* and *You run into each other at the delicatessen.*

"Now we need some really crummy, boring, rotten dates," said Park, warming up like a baseball pitcher and getting mean.

"I don't want that much reality," I protested. "This is a game. Suppose you're on a date and the car has a flat tire and the dog gets carsick and you miss the movie and you're late for your curfew and you get grounded for a month. You can't have a date like that in the game."

"Why not? It sounds perfect. Here. I'll put that down instead of *He has his own jet and takes you to Dallas.*"

Our heads came together over erasers and inks.

"Park?" I said, my nose next to his eraser.

"Yep?" He blew the eraser specks off where he was going to write; they dusted my face

"Do you think Wendy planned to break up with you, then? That she was just waiting for the moment she could blame it on you? Actually the breakup was kind of romantic, you know? 'Rescue by Jeep from the clutches of Park.' It's kind of like one of her soap scripts."

Park kept erasing. More slowly. He erased quite a few squares we hadn't discussed yet. I memorized them as they vanished so I could write them back later.

He sat up, stretched his legs, tucked them back, and began sorting through my boy cards. "These are good," he said in surprise. "Now, here you've got reality. Some boys are funny, some are fat. Some are rich and some have eight hundred zits." He read each card slowly.

I ought to have boys' opinions on my boy cards, I thought. Can't you just imagine me inviting Will and Jeep and Angie to come look at my romance game for me? Give me a few hints? Oh, right.

"When she was hitting me with her purse," said Parker, "she told me it was all an act. She never loved me."

Wendy carried a teeny purple leather purse: square, on a long, long, thin leather loop. The purse had exactly enough room for her driver's license and some cash. Pens and pencils she carried clipped to her notebook. Faith said once that there wasn't even room in that purse for Tampax. We decided that maybe Wendy didn't have periods. They weren't romantic enough.

I wanted to laugh insanely at the vision of Wendy whapping Parker with her miniature excuse for a purse; giving him miniature bruises.

But the bruise was enormous, and real.

"Her voice breaking on the phone with you?" I said. "Her hugging you and leaning on your shoulder? An act?" I considered going after her with a shotgun. Queen of Romance, indeed. She was Queen Bitch, if that was true.

The poster board slid from Parker's fingers and off the bed. It landed softly on my carpet, the huge heart sideways, and then it tipped facedown, so the hearts were hidden.

"That rotten, nasty, no-good—" I began.

"Don't say that." He wasn't ready to call Wendy names. He still loved her. She could be a rabid dog, and he still loved her.

Awful, awful, awful, I thought. Love is awful. Or Wendy is.

I put my arm around Park and he put his around me.

Not all love is romantic. Some is brother-and-sister love. Love is comfort.

8

♥ "All right, now this is important, Kelly. Tell your family to stay off the phone. You're going to get a call at ten o'clock, and we have to have all the details sorted out first so you don't screw up."

I was sound asleep. School had tired me out so much, I hadn't even gotten undressed but was sprawled over the covers, wrapped around my homework, with a pencil sticking in my side. "Megan?" I said groggily.

"That's right. Now, do you remember Richie?"

Richie. Nobody named Richie came to mind.

"I dated him in eighth grade. He's from Prospect Hill. There's a big dance Saturday night, and his girlfriend broke up with him and he called and asked me to go out, but I can't, I'm far too busy, so I gave him your number. I promised Richie you're good company, a great date, pretty, slender, and interested in sports."

"I'm slender anyway." I sat up. The ridges in my skin

from the bedspread felt an inch deep. I must have been asleep for ages.

"Do you have a formal gown or do you need to borrow one of mine?" Megan sounded so crisp, I wondered if she had a checklist in front of her. Steps to Take When Fixing Up Your Friend with Richie.

"I need to borrow one of yours." Megan had been to so many formal dances, she had a wardrobe of gowns, the way I have a wardrobe of T-shirts.

"Fine. Tomorrow after school. Now, be sure to joke a lot. He's a bad dancer; don't force him to dance. Be very relaxed. He's into sports, but he didn't make varsity basketball this season; don't mention basketball." Megan went on and on. I was dazed. How could I be relaxed when I had a forty-point checklist to follow?

"Richie is good stuff, Kelly. You don't want to mess up."

My hands were already sweaty, my dented cheeks feverish, and I hadn't even talked to Richie yet. I promised to be slender, pretty, interested in sports, and full of jokes.

My family is very nosy. I had no sooner hung up than Mother in her robe and Parker in his pajama bottoms were filling up my bedroom door, demanding to know what Megan wanted. Daddy would have been there, too, in the awful baggy gray sweat pants he wears to bed, but he was out. Whatever out meant. Mother was getting on his nerves something fierce. And the more she tried to relax, the more anxious she got, and the quicker he went out.

"What was that about?" Mother said. "Megan sounded like the end of the world. Is she running away from home or something?"

If Mother could offer Megan a home in time of crisis, it would certainly take her mind off Ellen and Daddy. "No,"

I said. "She's fixing me up with Richie, who needs a Saturday night dance date because his girlfriend walked out on him."

"Perfect for your romance game!" cried my mother. "Can't you see a whole life together built on the coincidence of Richie's girlfriend dumping him and you appearing in his life that very week?"

"How do you know about my board game?" I demanded.

"I *do* vacuum in here. You leave it out. Naturally my eyes landed on it. I think it's excellent."

"You snoop," I said indignantly.

"She isn't a snoop. You're just messy," said Parker. "And there is nothing romantic about this, Mother. Poor Richie gets dumped. He feels lower than low. He calls the only other girl he can think of, and Megan passes him on to a stranger like a helping of mashed potatoes. What's so romantic about that?"

"It is romantic potential," said my mother stiffly.

"Romance is a crock," said Parker.

The clock chimed ten downstairs, and the phone rang at precisely the same second. "He's punctual anyway," I said. "Go. Leave me alone. I cannot discuss anything with Richie with you two hovering over my bed."

"We're only going if you tell us the details afterward," said Parker.

"No. I'll never tell. And no fair listening through the crack." I shoveled them out, shut the door, retreated to the far side of the room, and still managed to get the phone on the fourth ring. "Hello?"

"May I speak to Kelly Williams, please?" A voice that sounded like a corpse.

"This is Kelly."

He didn't say anything more.

"Really," I said, remembering my order to joke. "It's true. This is Kelly."

He forced a laugh. "And this is Richie Devaney. Did—uh—did Megan—uh—"

I was thinking of Will. Would Will ever want to ask me out? Would going out with this stranger jeopardize that? But of course, Will would never know.

"Yes, Megan called," I said. I thought, I am insane. Worrying if I should stay loyal to Will? Will, who cares for me about one on a scale of one hundred? What is my *problem*? "And I'd love to go to the dance with you, Richie."

"Oh, great. Well. Uh." Richie was doing some very heavy breathing. I guess phone calls for blind dates come under the heading of strenuous exercise. "Thanks for bailing me out," he added in a rush.

"You're welcome." I struggled to think of something amusing, perhaps to do with his interest in sports, which would not place any demands on him, or . . . I gave up on that pretty fast. I gave him driving directions to my house instead.

"Oh, great. Well. Uh." Richie definitely had his one-syllable words down. "I'll pick you up at eight," he said, and we hung up.

Is it a bad sign that Megan was far too busy? I thought. With whom is she being so busy? Certainly not Jimmy. Certainly not Will.

I scooped up my board game. I put my finger on the Start Heart and slid myself slowly over the lacy pink line into the first square. "Romance," I told myself. "You asked for it, Kell, you got it."

♥

All week the dialogue repeated itself.

"Oooooh, I adore romance." That was Mother, of course.

"Poor pathetic Richie." That was Parker.

"My little girl, starting to get flowers of her own." That

was Daddy, listing possibilities for the corsage Richie would bring. "Carnations, orchids, roses, baby's breath. I can see them all out there, a whole greenhouse full, coming your way, Kelly." He was proud of me. As if he'd done something special, bringing Kelly up to swoon over flowers.

My mother wore a peculiar expression. And all of a sudden I didn't want any flowers. I didn't want to be like Mother, not feeling loved unless I had little gifts littering my life to prove it. I wanted love that was forgiveness and kindness and generosity and—

Will said all that, I thought.

And I wanted to call Will up and tell him about my parents' marriage: the most romantic marriage in Cummington—frail enough that a weekend a month away was tearing it apart. A marriage whose cement was Hallmark cards and silver violets.

Marriage, maybe, that had lasted eighteen years on romance—and not on love?

♥

My hair is slippery. Other girls with long hair can put it up in little braids and twists and interesting details. My hair just slides out, slithers down my cheek and neck, until there are a lot of pins sticking into the top of my head and all my hair is back where it started from. Flat, shiny, and smooth, as if it had never been disturbed.

"It's like a Law of Nature," said my mother, struggling to do something unique with it. "It never allows anything to interrupt its chosen path."

"Stop worrying," advised Parker. "All that Richie needs is a presentable female body walking in the door with him."

Daddy had brought me the present tonight: a gold charm to slip on my necklace. It wouldn't show, the way the

92

neckline of Megan's dress was cut, but that didn't matter. The charm was a tiny, delicate eighth note. "Because tonight is music," said my father, who was happier about my date with Richie than anybody, including me, "and because it's a prelude of things to come."

He sounded like a line off a greeting card. Were his gifts to Mother, his attentions to her, just a curtain to stand behind? Was he simply lubricating life so all things would go his way? And now Mother was demanding more: love and reassurance instead of plain old romance, and he did not have that to give?

"Park," said Daddy, "you sound as if you could use a presentable female body of your own."

"Yeah, well, I don't have an important affair on Saturday where I have to appear in public."

"There's the senior prom," I pointed out.

"Months away," Parker said.

"It's not that far off, Parker," said my mother. "My goodness, I wasn't thinking. How the calendar flies by. You'll have to put Wendy out of your mind and start dating other girls."

"If Park can put Wendy out of his mind," said my father. "How about you put Ellen out of your mind?"

We stood frozen in my room, framed against the pink bed and walls. Ellen was in there with us, and a million bouquets that meant nothing, and a future that frightened us all. I couldn't see my parents clearly. Daddy seemed oddly angry and menacing, instead of bear-hug cuddly. Mother shrank and turned wispy. Parker was not even there: reducing himself to shadow so he wouldn't have to participate.

Talk about it now, I prayed. Talk about how dumb this is. Admit Ellen doesn't matter. We do. We, the Williams family. Say you love each other.

But nobody said anything.

The doorbell rang. My father went downstairs to let Richie in, and Parker followed to take a look at Richie. Mother began folding things strewn around my room. She likes to fold. Making order out of chaos. So make some order out of *your* chaos, I thought. What is a sweatshirt on the floor compared to a marriage in shambles?

"Kelly, come on down," said my father loudly, with such gusto, he sounded like a quiz-show emcee.

I felt truly ill.

I swallowed, shivered, and went down.

Richie was very, very handsome.

I guess I thought he'd be a dud. But he looked wonderful! Megan was too busy to go out with *him*? He intimidated me just standing there. Just existing in all his poised male beauty. My steps faltered.

I was halfway down the stairs.

Richie said, "Oh, what a great dress!"

I relaxed. One compliment and I had my act together again. So this is why Mother needs compliments, I thought suddenly. You feel so much better! You feel so much more in control when somebody tells you you look good.

Richie took a single half-step toward me.

He was half smiling.

My mind, which moves at roughly the speed of light, whipped through the next five years. I took Richie through dating, being seniors together, going to both senior proms, college, and getting married. And I wasn't even at the bottom of the stairs yet.

"Kelly," he said, greeting me, but also confirming that he liked what he saw. If there was a test, I had passed his, and he had passed mine.

The room felt soft.

My parents seemed united and in love; wishing *me* love

perhaps. Parker was glad for me. Richie was relieved: Megan hadn't steered him wrong.

Ever so gently he slid a wrist corsage over my fingers and eased on the elastic strap so it didn't bite my skin. His hands held mine only for a moment, but it felt like the touch I had been waiting for all my life: concern and affection and interest and full of gifts to come.

And in the drive, waiting for us, was a long sleek black limousine.

My eyes met Mother's.

Her face was lit in sparkles, and she tilted her chin ever so slightly and pursed her lips in a tiny kiss to me. She was as thrilled as I was.

A dance.

A limousine.

A nosegay of flowers on my wrist and a handsome boy in a dark, romantic suit.

"Good night," I said to my family. Even my voice felt softer, my hand already in Richie's. He was no stranger; his clasp was warm and strong, as if he, too, had been waiting for this hand, this moment.

I smiled at Richie and he smiled back, and for an instant we paused in the door, already caught in romance.

I heard a sigh.

Park. A sigh for love and its joys.

But tonight it was my turn.

9

♥ The limousine returned me home at a quarter to midnight.

It was the driver, and not Richie, who walked me to the front door.

I was much earlier than my family had expected. When Daddy opened the door, he was astonished, and then upset, thinking something was wrong. I went in quickly, shutting the door hard, blocking away the vision and the memory of Richie Devaney.

"Kell?" said Daddy worriedly.

I meant to go straight to my room. Be like Parker, and tell nothing. But unlike Parker, I couldn't bear it; I told Daddy all. It was a quick sentence.

"He didn't like me, Daddy."

Parents can't tolerate that kind of sentence. "Of course, he did, Kelly. He was probably just shy."

"No, Daddy. He didn't like me. He didn't try to talk or get to know me. I was just a stuffed doll he towed around so he wouldn't be alone at the dance. He propped me up in front of his friends, and especially his old girlfriend, but I wasn't special enough for that. He needed somebody really dazzling and I'm not dazzling. I'm just an ordinary pretty girl. I disappointed him."

My father picked me up.

He hadn't held me sitting on his lap, my head on his shoulder, since I was little. My tears soaked into his heavy woolen sweater. My lovely long gown was caught between us, dragging behind like torn rags. I pulled off the wrist corsage and let it fall. All that was left of the evening was a painful red mark where the corsage band had gripped me all night.

Daddy dropped, still holding me in his arms, into his recliner. It's not a chair I like: too big, too ugly—but oh, it was a comfort. Both of us tilted back. I sobbed on Daddy as if I were really his little girl still.

All my life I've wanted to grow up. Stop playing games. Have the real thing.

But the real thing hurt.

The real thing was being ignored. Not measuring up. Not being talked to. Not being danced with. "Daddy, I thought it would be so perfect. It was all there. Flowers and a limousine and music and a handsome boy."

"Aw, Kell." Daddy shifted me around so I was sitting next to him, my head next to his on the leather pillow. We stared at the oil painting of the sea and the sand my mother bought years ago on their honeymoon: the view from their hotel. "Don't hate romance," said my father. "I'm really into romance. I think it's neat."

"Not for me it isn't."

"Don't write it off just because of one lousy boy, one lousy night."

97

"But, Daddy, it was my first date! And what if it's my *only* date?"

"First dates are hard," he agreed. "Takes practice to figure out what you're doing."

"Richie has had lots of practice," I said miserably. "And he didn't want to do anything with me but have me there."

"But he was so nice when he picked you up!" protested my father.

He had been showing off. All night long, Richie Davaney showed off. But not to me. To my family, to the chauffeur whose services he engaged back when he was still going with Jill—that was her name, Jill; she was just like Wendy: a queen of romance—he showed off to his friends, to his teachers, to the chaperons, and most of all, to Jill.

But he didn't show off to me.

I wasn't worth it.

"The flowers were just flowers and the music was just notes," I said. "I was another purchase, like the corsage. But less successful."

Daddy smoothed my hair: always silken, always soft. Hair I had wanted Richie to touch. "If he's that dumb, who needs him?" said my father.

"*I* need him. I want a boyfriend."

"Your time will come."

"Daddy, I can't *stand* it when you say that. I don't want my time to arrive out there in the future when I'm old. I want it right now! In high school, my junior year, right this minute! I want it like Megan has it, and Wendy has it, and the way you and Ellen used to have it."

Oh, was I sorry I said that!

Now even my misery was ruined. I had to think of my parents' misery as well. I couldn't even wallow in my own disaster.

"Sweetie, I learned a lot in those eight years with Ellen," said my father after a long, sad pause. "You know I'm addicted to buying stuff. I just love to give presents. If I'm working all day, and it's rotten, and I have to be nice to people I hate, or work on a project I think is stupid, or finish one I think needs another six weeks, it's so nice to be able to do something right. Buy a long-stemmed red rose, hand it to your mother, and see her light up. And I found out from Ellen that you can run a long, long time on that. It can fuel years of dating."

The last thing I wanted was a heart-to-heart talk about Ellen. I wanted to talk about *me*. Was that so selfish? Once in sixteen years? To want him to focus on *me*?

"But it can't supply love," finished my father.

Had Daddy bought Ellen? The way Richie bought me? Flowers and music and sleek cars? And had Ellen let it go eight years because she liked dating, she liked the attention— but she didn't love him, and never had?

And incredibly it was Ellen I agreed with. I wanted to flirt, and be liked, and have presents, and dance gracefully with the handsome boy. I hadn't asked Richie to love me. Just to have fun being with me.

And he couldn't bother.

I wasn't worth it.

I was worth nothing.

I began crying horribly.

"You matter to me," said Daddy.

Every father in the world, and every mother, has tried to end a talk with that line. You matter to *me*, dear. *I* love you. So what if there's not a boy on earth who does? Your old daddy loves you, and that's what counts, huh?

"You just have to get through it, Kell," he said, hugging me fiercely. "You'll feel better eventually and manage to stand up again, and there will be somebody there, I guarantee it."

"But, Daddy, some girls never find anybody. I don't want to be like them. I don't want to be a loser."

"Of course not. Everybody hates being a loser."

"It's worse than that. Everybody hates the loser, too, and they don't associate with her, and then she's even *more* of a loser."

The kitchen chime-clock struck the quarter hour, and after a long silence, the half hour. My father's breathing was so regular, I thought he might have gone to sleep. The tears had dried on my cheeks, and their tracks were itchy. My dress was caught up under me awkwardly and I wanted to yank it around so it wouldn't pull at my skin.

"I'm getting all stiff, Daddy. And I'm wrinkling the dress. I guess I'll go on to bed."

He tilted the recliner forward, and it half flung me onto my feet. "I didn't have any words of wisdom, did I?" said my father sadly. "I'm sorry. I wanted to help."

"The only thing that could help right now would be the phone ringing and some terrific boy telling me he adores me and he can't go another twenty-four hours without seeing me."

My father began laughing. "I could pay somebody off," he suggested.

"You stinker. That's like Megan fixing me up. I want it just to *come*. Like a door opening. Fireworks exploding."

I could see it both ways.

A door: a glimpse into an unknown room, and the unknown boy who would love me.

Fireworks: seeing this boy, falling apart inside, and coming together on the surface—explosions and fire and laughter and joy.

100

"God, you're like your mother," said my father, so exasperated—and so filled with love.

I was really annoyed with him. Me—like mother? Eternally anxious? Hiding from reality? Busying herself with nothing much? Only smiling when Daddy smiled first?

Me?

"Kelly," said my father softly, "it's okay to be needy. It's okay to need love. You don't have to be sorry you need it. You don't have to fight back, Kell."

10

♥ "Kelly," said Megan, "you are blind. You need a guide dog for dating."

I didn't cry or anything. I was proud of my self-control. At least she didn't tell me I'm the dog, I thought. I washed my hands. The school has gray soap in the girls' rooms. I don't think a person can get clean with gray soap. It's a contradiction.

Megan sagged down the wall of the girls' room, sinking dramatically onto the tile floor. Her hair draped over some of the obscene graffiti.

"Don't do that," said Faith crossly. "They haven't mopped in here since Carter was President." Faith brushed her hair with such vigor that I cringed. If I were that rough, I'd shortly be bald, along with all my other troubles. Faith never even notices the handfuls of hair she loses; she just fills the wastebaskets and moans about humidity.

"Here I kill myself to arrange the perfect evening for

you, Kelly, with Richie, who is also perfect, and you screw up."

"Oh, Megan, don't yell at me," I said. Tears crawled closer to the surface. "Don't tell me I screwed up. Tell me we just weren't right for each other."

Megan drummed her heels against the tiles. She was wearing good shoes with tiny sharp metal points on the high heels. She lifted her knees ever so slightly so she could do a sitting-down tap dance. I was filled with admiration for her coordination. "Kelly, you should not get so emotional," said Megan. "It was only a date. Nothing but a dance. You should have laughed your way through a great evening. You're too intense. You cannot, cannot, cannot be intense about boys."

Then what's the point? I thought. Who needs it if it's not intense?

Faith said mournfully, "I'm awfully emotional about Angie. Do you think that's why he doesn't respond? We had such fun at lunch!" A lunch that by now had to have been a month ago. "We flirted and giggled and joked, and it was perfect. So why won't he ask me out?"

Megan heaved a huge sigh. She began explaining in details why Faith and I were failures in love. At first I listened because I really wanted to know, but about ten syllables in I saw it was going to be too depressing, so I checked out. Megan punctuated her lecture with heel taps. She was ruining her shoes, getting scuff marks all over them. She didn't care. No boy would care either.

I stared at myself in the mirror. All the bathrooms at Cummington High are gray. There was probably some unbelievable sale on gray tiles and gray sinks when they were building the school. I'm happy they saved all that money, but I know now I'll pick my college on the basis of

103

bathroom color. I am tired of feeling gray inside, and then being reflected in gray on the outside as well.

I was even wearing gray. My oldest sweatshirt, the baggy one with the words so faded, even I am not sure what they say. My oldest jeans: so pale now, they're a reflection of my personality—Pretend jeans covering a pretend girl.

If we stay in this bathroom much longer, I thought, I'm going to have a nervous breakdown. Maybe I'm *already* having a nervous breakdown.

Faith said, "I'm having a nervous breakdown over Angie, and he doesn't even know it. I think of him every minute. Setting the table or doing math or watching cable or practicing the flute, and Angie is part of it. It's as if his invisible clone is stuck to me. Some terrible glue I can never melt."

I should add that to my board game, I thought. *Pointless Crush. Total Obsession. Unrequited Love.*

Megan took about fifteen paper towels to dry her hands. One high school junior gets clean, and the wastebasket is overflowing.

"It's my name," said Faith glumly. "I have this overwhelming need to be faithful. To have one guy in my life and love him forever."

Megan shuddered. "You're right. You're doomed. *They'll* never feel that way. If *you* do, it's over."

She made it sound as if we came in one dimension: pretty paper dolls, all equal.

"Let's go," said Faith. "Sociology next. We don't want to be late. Maybe Angie will ask me for lunch again today."

And maybe not.

Angie. Perhaps it was Angie who was one-dimensional. His expression never changed, his charm never dwindled. But what was inside him really? Anything at all? Was Faith in love with nothing?

Perhaps love itself was nothing.

The other two hurtled toward sociology. I trudged. Me—with my romance obsession—wondering if love itself was nothing.

At least it put me in control of my emotions. I hadn't seen Will since the dance with Richie. Now that I knew love was nothing, boys were paper dolls, and I needed a guide dog, I certainly wouldn't have a crush on Will. I probably wouldn't even recognize Will.

That made me feel much better. Strong. Independent. Calm and poised.

In the doorway to Miss Simms's class stood Will.

The face that had seemed just bony now was full of interesting angles and planes. The eyebrows that turned his expression to conceit seemed inquisitive, interested. The face that seemed snobbish was instead stranded—somebody needing a friend.

Will looked at the three of us.

Vibrant Megan.

Faith radiating her crush on Angie.

And me. My sloppiest sweatshirt. My grayest emotions.

"How are you, Kelly?" said Will, as if Megan and Faith were invisible.

"William, William, you're blocking the road," said Megan, who cannot bear to be ignored, and certainly not by a boy she just ignored herself.

"Fine, thanks, Will," I told him.

He nodded, and went back to his seat.

Only people who have suffered from really serious crushes—terminal crushes—know you can be wafted off for an entire class on a "How are you?" and a nod.

Music to my ears.

I was wearing one nice thing: my gold chain with the

gold charm—a tiny eighth note. I fingered it while I looked at Will, hoping for a glance or a smile that would confirm his interest. Prove he wasn't snubbing Megan, but he was crazy about me. Will's interest was in the lecture. He took notes and never looked up.

I really care, I thought. Oh, not so much about Will. Will and Richie hardly even matter. I just want somebody to like me. I don't care any more who does the liking.

I am desperate.

What a terrible word in a girl's vocabulary.

". . . to be special," squeaked Miss Simms. "You do research—library work—in English and history. Translation papers in Spanish and French. Laboratory research in biology and chemistry. But for your sociology project, I want something special. Anything to do with the way one person interacts with another."

"Can it be the way boy interacts with girl?" piped up Angie.

"Of course! Male-female relationships are very complex. Any data you can supply to help us understand will be greatly appreciated."

Angie beamed. "Then my project's finished. I've been working on it since my thirteenth birthday, and I've already—"

"I think not, Angelo," said Miss Simms. "Sexual expertise"—she smiled suddenly, more amused than the situation seemed to call for—"or the lack thereof, will not be considered."

Why, he's all show! I thought. The realization shocked me. He's been hiding from himself and fooled everyone. Except Miss Simms. I smiled. Miss Simms knows it: It isn't that the girls don't measure up to Angie's standards—it's that Angie doesn't know what to do next. I really wanted to tell Faith, but maybe I was wrong. I needed time to think. I tuned into Miss Simms's voice again.

"Project ideas must be submitted within two weeks. If you are late, the grade will drop ten percent."

Lots of people take sociology as a gut course to keep their grade levels high. Now they'd have to exert themselves, which caused class-wide groaning. Even Wendy whined. "But Miss Simms, I do so *much* creative stuff *already*! I don't have *time* to think up something *else* that's special and wonderful."

This time Will did look my way. We rolled our eyes at each other. Did Wendy Newcombe have a high opinion of herself!

Jeep spoke up on Wendy's behalf, wanting Wendy to be exempt from the project—or be allowed to submit a soap script! Parker would do that, too, I thought. He's still on Wendy's team, even though I don't think she has a team: She's captain for herself alone.

I should put *that* on the board too. A square to show that *sometimes you love a person for what doesn't exist*! You'd have to have a big board-penalty for that.

Of course, you didn't need a board game to pay penalties. All you had to do was fall in love.

Romance.

Such a soft and beautiful word. Such hard, cruel parts within it.

And suddenly I was laughing—almost exulting! My romance game! That would be my sociology project! A class activity. Male-female relationships and the complexity thereof. Miss Simms would love it!

The bell rang; the class vanished, I struggled to my feet. You would think, skinny as I am, that I could come up out of a school desk like an eel through the water, but I must have the wrong proportions. Never once have I stood up gracefully in school.

"I am dying to know what you're thinking," said Will, standing next to me. "The expressions that have crossed your face in the last five minutes have been priceless. The trouble is, I didn't figure out a single one."

I blushed to imagine my face. "Hard to explain," I mumbled. And immediately regretted it. Megan was right. I *did* need a guide dog to dating. I sounded as if I didn't want to talk to him.

"Wendy's kind of a jerk, isn't she?" observed Will, going with me to the door.

"I love hearing you say that," I exclaimed. "You're so removed and objective. If you say she's a jerk, then she is."

"Me? Removed?" It surprised him. I didn't know what to say to explain it that wouldn't be half insulting, so I didn't say anything. I just blushed away, a whole sentence of blushing.

We reached the hall.

Will said, "I'm sure your expressions meant something interesting. Would you tell me over a Coke? This afternoon?"

11

♥ If only I had on the right clothes!

Something to show off my figure (such as it is). Good color, good lines, and great jewelry to top it.

But no. I was in my oldest jeans, where parts of the side seams have split, so there are indigo-blue stripes down my legs. I couldn't even take off my old gray sweatshirt, because underneath I had on a jersey just for the collar—the rest of the shirt was bleach-stained and torn.

And that's what I had to wear on my first real date. (Richie didn't count. He was more a punishment. For both of us.)

But Will was a date.

And I was afraid of him.

Afraid! But I'd known Will most of my life. Watched him in sports, where conceit serves him so well, and disliked him in class, where conceit is so infuriating. What was there to be afraid of?

I dawdled.

He was waiting for me in the front foyer. Why wasn't I running to him, the way Wendy ran after Parker, was running now toward Jeep? I wanted this so much: a boy asking for my company. And now it had come, and the boy was truly fantastic . . . and I was dragging my feet.

A thousand times I'd listened to Megan about her boyfriends. Never once had fear come into the conversation. Desire, worry, adoration, frustration, concern—but not fear.

"Hi," said Will, grinning.

There was certainly no fear visible in Will. Will is so tall that merely to be there is a display. I felt as if the entire school were watching me go up to him, saw my head tilt back to greet him. I had always figured I would love being on parade. But I was shrinking back, wishing we could be alone, in private. Afraid of being overheard or seen.

"Hi," I said, and I blushed and looked away from him. Over a "hi," which I say to a hundred people, including Will, every single day!

"Let's go to Wendy's," said Will.

I was truly shocked. *Wendy's?* But surely Will knew she'd been so mean to my brother. Surely the two of us had agreed just that day that Wendy was a pain. Was the whole basketball team going out with Wendy? Was this a double date with Jeep? Was—

"Wendy's the hamburger place," said Will. "Did you really think I meant Wendy Newcombe's?"

"I guess she's on my mind."

"She doesn't deserve the space. Come on. My car's in the east lot because I was late this morning. We have to hike."

We didn't touch. We didn't even walk very close. And in spite of the fact that I was afraid, I was disappointed. As long as you're doing it, you should do it, right? Tons of people were looking at us, or at least facing our way. I wanted to give them something to look at.

Boy, am I sitting on both sides of *this* fence! I thought. How do I expect Will to have any idea what I'm thinking when *I* don't have any idea what I'm thinking?

My mind split.

Rushing down the paths of other minds, wondering what they were thinking, and thinking for them. My father's path, my mother's, Parker's, Wendy's, Faith's, Megan's— seeing with their eyes, deciding with their minds.

I've always wondered if other people's minds do that: divide, splinter, race headlong in multiples.

Or do other people always know who they are?

"You know, Kelly, I've come to a conclusion about you," said Will.

"What's that?"

"I figured you for solid as a rock, but now I think you're kind of flaky—a space cadet. A lot of girls, I psych them out, I know who they are, and I get bored. With you I have this feeling that you don't land. You only *look* as if you land. But really you're flying out there somewhere and you've *never* landed."

"I didn't know you thought about me at all." It was a queer, glorious feeling, to imagine myself in Will's thoughts: to imagine that when his mind split, one of the paths it took was through me.

"A person has to think of something during sociology," Will pointed out. "I've been working my way through all the girls in the class. Depends which way I'm facing. Like when I was facing Wendy, I spent a lot of time trying to figure out what game she's been playing with Jeep and Parker."

"Oh, me too. I'd give anything to understand that."

111

Will opened the car door for me. I love that. I have hard-line feminist friends who can't stand it, won't let it happen, but I think it's just courtesy and has nothing to do with important issues like equal pay. I love little attentions.

Little attentions.

My mind slipped; the gears shifted; I saw the thousand little attentions Daddy gave Mother. For the millionth time in a month I wondered about my parents. I prayed they weren't getting a—

And for the first time the real word crept into my mind. *Divorce.*

Horrible, evil word. I let it sit quietly in my mind, and then I picked it up, like a stone, and flung it away, as far away as I could.

Will walked around the car and got in his side. He put the key in and the car began buzzing horribly. "Put your seat belt on," he yelled.

I snapped it in place. "My goodness. Our car has a sweet, tinkling bell for seat belts. Yours gets violent."

He started the engine. "Tell me why you'd give anything to understand Wendy. I'm not sure Wendy is worth understanding."

"Because of Parker. She really hurt him."

"I'll bet. We could see it coming, but Park couldn't. One of those things where you couldn't warn him or you'd be the enemy. You just had to wait, and then when he's ready, we can go in and maybe pick up a few of the pieces."

"Parker's not letting anybody pick up the pieces."

Will nodded. "I think most boys feel that way. You don't go around begging for understanding. You pull yourself together. I meant more that his friends are there, and Park knows it."

"Will you ever talk about it with him?" I asked.

"Doubt it."

Our girl talks, all on that pink ribcord bedspread. Intimate and heartbreaking or silly and giggly. We told all. We loved telling all. We would always tell all.

Or so I thought until I fell for Will. I hadn't told anybody that. Not even Faith. For some reason *especially* not even Faith.

I wasn't afraid of Will any more. Talking had released the fear.

We arrived at Wendy's and got in line. For the first time Will touched me, his hand on my waist. Not light, not a half tickle, but a firm palm that ushered me ahead of him. I asked for chili; he ordered four hot dogs.

"Four?" I said.

"I don't know why hot dogs are made so skinny. A person has to eat a whole package to be satisfied."

I laughed.

Any remaining tension oozed out of me. This wasn't going to be scary or demanding. We were going to chatter easily, and I was going to enjoy myself thoroughly and that would be that. Still smiling, I turned to gaze up at him. He was looking down at me speculatively, the way I might look at a dress I'm thinking of buying, but haven't definitely decided on.

Nervousness came back like a blow.

Getting and losing points.

Will's hand moved me forward again. The tray was handed over the counter, and Will took it. One hand holding the tray, the other still resting on my waist, he walked us toward a table at the window on the far side.

No wonder my mother loved all the little things Daddy did. They made you feel special. And who could not want that? It's terrific to feel you're worth an effort to somebody.

113

My thoughts split again, abandoning my date. Opening doors, holding the tray, choosing the table: I knew I enjoyed this, so what could be wrong with it? What were Parker and I thinking of? Knocking Daddy for showing Mother affection that way? And what were Mother and Daddy thinking of? Letting it fade so fast? Over *Ellen*. Whom nobody cared about.

The letter. Did Daddy still have Ellen's letter in his wallet? Was he still staring at her photograph? Was he sorry he was married to Mother? Was he planning to—

"Now you *have* to tell me that one," said Will. "This time I refuse to be left in the dark."

"That what?" I said, though I knew perfectly well.

"That thought. Another intense one." He took all the food off the tray and slid the tray onto a vacant table behind us. Handing me a napkin and a straw, he got to work on hot dog number one.

It took him three bites and maybe fifteen seconds to eat the whole thing. He washed it down with about half his soda without pausing for breath.

I was still lifting my spoon to approach the chili.

"Wow," I said.

Will grinned. "I eat kind of fast."

"I guess you do."

"But that doesn't let you off the hook. What were you thinking about that made you look so far off?"

I put the white plastic spoon into the chili, brought up a mouthful, and lowered it back down. I picked up a pack of crackers, although I don't like crackers and never spoil my chili with them. I played with the cellophane.

"That heavy?" said Will.

"It's my parents. I thought they had the most beautiful marriage on earth. I loved thinking about the way they lived

114

together, and how someday I would live like that. And now—for the smallest, dumbest reasons—it's coming apart at the seams. Parker and I are kind of standing there watching it split. Little teeny things keep happening and yet it's been so *fast,* Will! As though it never had much strength after all, when we thought it was the strongest in Cummington. Sometimes just one word in an ordinary conversation makes me remember. I get scared."

Will touched my hand. The cellophane of the crackers rustled at the pressure. I looked at his hand. It dwarfed mine. It was like my father's hand: enormous, two of mine. He left it on my skin: two fingertips pressing on me. It was comforting out of all proportion to what he was touching.

"My folks are divorced and remarried and divorced again. You live through it. I won't say it's a picnic, but eventually everybody comes out on the side without being destroyed."

"I don't want to think about it. I can't *bear* thinking about it."

He nodded. "I don't imagine they want to think about it either."

"I am sure if my mother would just act like an adult, it could all be solved in a weekend."

"What's she doing?" And then without the slightest break added, "Are you going to eat those crackers or not? The sound of cellophane is starting to get to me, lady. So make up your mind."

I was almost hurt. I *was* hurt. I had come very close to telling Will what I hadn't even told Parker: my ultimate fears. And he interrupted that to talk cellophane?

Jeep said, "Hey, you two, why didn't you say you were coming over here? Hi, Kell. Shove over, will you?"

He and Wendy, arms around each other, faces full of

love and laughter, were bouncing beside us. Oh, truly the *last* girl on earth I would want to have hear my problems! I sent Will a look of heartfelt relief. His eyelids closed slightly, and he nodded infinitesimally, and I knew he had interrupted our conversation on purpose to save me.

"No," said Wendy. "Kelly, you change seats and sit next to Will so I can sit with Jeep."

I in my nasty sweatshirt, Wendy in a perfect outfit: as if she were the star of her soap, not the writer. Setting fashion trends, staring into cameras. Her laugh was musical, her complexion perfect, and Jeep's hand was locked around her waist.

Will gave me an I'm-on-your-team smile.

I got up, feeling like a stick figure wearing rags, and crept around the table to the other seat. Will slid my chili, drink, and crackers to my new place while Jeep and Wendy arranged themselves across from us. I hated it. I wanted to look at Will, not this pair.

Wendy was already talking, having chosen the subject and not the least bit interested in what we might have been talking about. Just as well, but still offensive. "I've decided to have the rest of the action for next week's soap in an amusement park. Jeep's recorded some great honky-tonk music for the merry-go-round, and we've got some wonderful screams for the roller coaster. I think I'm going to have the Ferris wheel break and Octavia fall off."

"Poor Octavia," I said. "She just recovered from her pregnancy. Now she's going to fall a hundred feet to a hideous, splatty death next to the cotton candy? Don't do that, Wendy."

"Oooooh, I love it," said Wendy to Jeep, and Jeep only. They squeezed a kiss in between sentences. "Kelly takes this stuff seriously. She's really worried. I love that, Jeep."

Wendy's a piece of paper, I thought. She's not a script

116

writer, she's a script herself. She doesn't care about Parker or me or even Octavia. She just cares about her effect on the world.

"Do you realize that when you're having these heavy thoughts," said Will, "your mouth opens slightly and your eyes slip out of focus?"

"She doesn't have heavy thoughts," giggled Wendy, "she's just got a weak jaw."

"Hey," I said indignantly.

"Watch it, Wendy Woman," said Will, "or I'll pour chili on your cute little blouse."

"It *is* a nice blouse, isn't it?" said Wendy contentedly.

Will and I burst out laughing.

Will ate two more hot dogs, which kept him busy for about as many minutes, finished his soda, and looked longingly at mine. "Yes," I told him. He nodded happily and drank half of it.

"I just want to go on record as saying I stand in awe of your hot-dog eating capacity," I said. "I am truly impressed."

"And to think I've been trying to show off by getting A's, or getting baskets. All I had to do was have my usual afternoon snack." He ate the fourth hot dog. "There. Now I feel like a human being again. Person needs sustenance to keep up human beingness."

"It *is* harder for you than for most of us," agreed Wendy.

"How come you don't like me?" complained Will.

"Because you're conceited," she told him.

"*I'm* conceited?" he snorted.

Will and I laughed together, but I think we were laughing at different things. I would stack Wendy's conceit next to anybody's, and put money on it, but a month ago I would have said the same of Will.

"Now I'm all sad," said Will.

117

"Because you have a stomachache from eating four hot dogs?" asked Wendy.

"Sad because they're gone. I love to eat. Wish I could make every meal last hours." His face grew wistful, and he eyed his crumbs as if wondering whether to pick them up and eat them too.

"I know this is not a very high-tech solution," I said, putting my hand on his, "but you could try taking smaller bites."

We all laughed.

Wendy went back to her favorite topic (Wendy), and we listened. It dawned on me that Jeep was not talking. He was sitting there, handsome as handsome could ever be: handsome as a—

As a soap-opera star. But that was it. Wendy was living out her own soap opera. Jeep was her male lead. And Park was—what? Her experiment? Her twist in the plot?

Into my ear Will murmured, "You really have to control your face, Kell. It's impossible to tell what you're thinking, but you're definitely thinking something we'd all like to tune in on."

He was breathing against my cheek and ear and hair. It made me shiver. When I turned to smile, our faces were nearly touching. Within a fraction of an inch. I was aware of freckles I'd never seen, lashes I'd never noticed, flecks in his hazel eyes I hadn't identified. Had never cared about.

And now cared so intensely about, I had to look away.

I hadn't even started my chili.

What expressions is my face giving away now? I thought, plummeting off some cliff, falling so much harder for Will than I'd expected. Am I going to have to bring along a mirror to study myself in? So I can keep a mask on?

"Come along, George Peters," said Wendy. "Let's move

on!" She turned to us. "Things to do, people to see." She took his hand and they almost danced out.

"Aren't people mysterious?" I said.

"There's nothing mysterious about those two. Wendy wants to run the world and Jeep's willing to be run."

Surely the most romantic-looking couple in Cummington High. A lot of people were glad when Wendy went back to Jeep. It looked better, they said. Parker just wasn't her type. She and Jeep are so romantic.

But what was romantic about Wendy and Jeep? Nothing, by my definition. Everything, by theirs.

Will was talking basketball. "We're in a strange battle between our two coaches. The head coach says it's enough to do your best; you don't have to win. The assistant coach says that winning is the only thing that counts, ever." He twirled my chili bowl. "You going to eat this?"

"No. Have it."

He ate my chili between sentences. "When we're practicing, I can agree with the head coach. You do your best, you're proud, and it *is* enough." He opened the crackers and added them to the remains of the chili. But when we're actually in a game, all I care about is winning." He finished the chili. "I love to win," he said softly, his voice as intense as Wendy on her soaps. "Winning is everything."

Winning.

The purpose behind every game, every crossword puzzle, every contest, every video game. Every race and every argument.

"What is winning?" I said.

"Being first," said Will, without having to wonder.

I didn't have a winning streak or much desire for one. It was okay with me to get average grades; I didn't have to be on honor roll. It was okay with me to coast downhill; I didn't have to ride my bike in races.

But now, for the first time, I wanted to be first.

First with Will.

"I'd like to win the state championship and enough points to have my sweatshirt retired in the glass trophy case in the front foyer," said Will. He smiled: a smile to hide a kind of sadness. "And what do you want to win, Kelly Williams?"

"Happily Ever After."

I was so surprised I'd said it out loud. Oh, no! I thought, did I really say that? To Will?

But he didn't laugh. He didn't get up and leave. "Oh, wow," he said, and this time the smile was sympathetic. "I've seen a lot of divorce in my family. I guess I don't have much faith in happily ever after. A girl who wants that—she wants it all."

"But you see, I thought I had it all. Or at least, I thought my parents did."

"Maybe they do. Maybe this is just a temporary lapse."

Temporary lapse.

And what was this afternoon with Will? I wondered as he drove me home, enjoying the traffic as much as his passenger. Was this real? Will it go somewhere? Or is it a temporary lapse?

12

♥ You could look at me and see.

I didn't see it. I wore my favorite outfit, but when I looked in the mirror to check it, I didn't see any difference.

In first period Faith said, "You look all sparkly, Kelly."

"I do?" I thought, Do I want to say *It's Will—I'm in love—we had a Coke—I want him to ask me out?* I said, "Maybe it's my blouse. This is my best color, you know."

Megan looked sharply at the blouse. "I suppose. But Faith's right, Kell. You seem bouncier than usual."

"I had a good night's sleep."

What a lie.

I hardly slept at all the night after Will and I went for chili.

Instead, I lay there, thinking alternately of him and me, layering us like lasagna: first the pasta, then the sauce. First Kelly, then Will, then Kelly, then Will, until they were one.

Forget taking me skiing in Colorado, Will. Skip the cruise to the Bahamas. Just telephone me. That's all I ask.

At around three in the morning I got out my romance game.

By now I had worked out a name system so you didn't draw a boy or a girl card, but got a *blank* card. You had to fill in the name before you started, and as you played you landed on squares that built the character of your date by chance.

I named my date Will.

Immediately chance turned him into a slob who had bad breath, drove a rusted-out station wagon, and worked at a landfill for a living.

"Well, that's no fun," I said irritably.

So this time I gave myself *four* dates to take around the board and I named them all Will: Will One, Will Two, Will Three, Will Four.

And this time the game worked!

The way a game should!

It was dumb, it sailed, it was funny, it made me giggle.

Will One never took me on a date. I'm sure he would have if he could, but Will One never landed on a date square. My game rule is that you can't arrive at Happily Ever After with somebody you've never dated, so that got rid of Will One.

Will Two was rich, which was nice, but he was bald, which was not. Will Two, in spite of being addicted to TV reruns, bought me a ski lodge and flowers.

Now, Will Three never developed any character at all. He dated me five times, so I could definitely go to Happily Ever After with him, but who wants a future with a personality-free man?

Will Four.

Now, there was a man a girl could love. He was thoughtful, the board informed me, had high-voltage sex appeal, was a rock star, had long blond hair, and never complained. His only vice was that he slept with four dogs. Oh, well, I told myself, it's probably a big bed. And I can get used to the dogs.

I knew Will Four was the man for me when *Your date composes a love song just for you* appeared in his cards.

I played slowly, hoping Will One would take me on at least one date and that Will Two would land on a *Lose all vices; now your date is perfect* square.

At four in the morning I landed on a Broken Heart.

> *Just like life!*
> *With no explanation whatsoever*
> *Your date dumps you for good.*
> *Cry all night.*

A nasty jagged lightning streak ripped through the red heart, leaving one half bleeding on the ground. Land on that square, and your date is off forever.

Whatever number I rolled would now be the number of the date that dumped me with no explanation.

If I rolled Will One, it wouldn't matter, because he never took me out anyhow. If I rolled Will Two, I could shrug. Will Three had yet to develop personality, so presumably I wouldn't notice. But Will Four. What if I rolled Four? That meant I'd have to keep playing the game with the other, lesser Wills, and end up at Happily Ever After with one of them—or with nobody.

For some time I jiggled the die in my palm.

Talk about superstition. I would have said I don't have a superstitious bone in my body. Certainly not while playing a board game that *I* invented, for heaven's sake.

But I never rolled that die. At four fifteen in the morning, I was much too exhausted to stay awake another second. I set the game back under the bed, dropped the die on the floor, turned out my light, and never knew which Will would have bitten the dust if I'd rolled one more turn.

But I did obey the square.

I cried myself to sleep.

I don't even know why. The tears came, and they were no soft, salty streaks on my cheeks, but terrible, bitter sobs, as if something dreadful had happened and I just hadn't been told yet.

But all things are better in the morning.

I woke up happy, even if I'd had only three hours sleep. I dressed eagerly, glad to be able to atone for my baggy sweatshirt of the day before: a plum-colored shirt with a deep teal-blue belt over it. The colors are hot and exciting against my gold hair. I could hardly wait to get to school.

School would not be a board game. It was the real thing.

A real Will, who really enjoyed me. Who really sat across from me in sociology and had a real personality.

I planned out how I'd enter the room. After Will, not before. I'd be with Faith, although she wouldn't know she was an escort. I'd be very casual. Then I'd smile. Our eyes would meet. We'd have a secret: interest in each other.

Maybe he'd pass me a note when Miss Simms was hidden behind her papers. Maybe I'd send him one. Maybe he'd say, "That shirt is a great color on you." Maybe he'd write, "Listen, I have fifteen minutes after school, before practice. Meet me in the student lounge."

I bounded down to breakfast—and a mother and father who were not speaking to each other. Whatever fight they'd had was over. They were in a state of truce. Or else putting up a front with me there.

My mother said, "Eggs, Kelly?"

My father said, "Orange juice, Kelly?"

My mother said, "Your father will drive you to school, Kelly."

My father said, "I don't believe I offered to do that, Violet."

They looked at each other. My parents, who never glare, were absolutely expressionless. Each was choking back words. And doing it well. As if they'd had lots of practice.

Had this been going on for ages? And I just never noticed?

"I can take the bus," I said quickly. Parker must have gotten an early ride with friends. There was no sign of him.

"You're late. He'll drive you," said my mother. Her jaw was set so tightly, it hurt my own jaw to see her teeth.

"No, it's okay, really. The bus is fine."

"Whose side are you on?" screamed my mother.

We weren't even having an argument. I didn't even *care* how I got to school.

"She's not on a side, Violet," said my father. "There *are* no sides. Can you please grow up?"

"Can *I* grow up?" repeated my mother icily. "I believe the shoe is on the other foot, George."

Horrible, thick silence while they both choked back again.

"What shoe?" I said. "What are we talking about?" Don't keep this up, I prayed. I want to think about Will. I want to think about love. I want to think about dates and flirting, not if you two . . . if you—

"I have no idea," said my father. "Get in the car. I'm taking you to school."

"I have a meeting tonight," said my mother. "I won't be home for dinner, George."

"Neither will I."

They both shrugged. They'd been married so long, their shrugs were identical, but they didn't notice. Only I did. I wanted to shrug, too, but I had no practice. I ran after Daddy.

In the car I said, "What's happening, Daddy?"

"Let's see. I'm going to pick up the newspaper, go to work, and after that I'm going duckpin bowling with Charlie and Frank. Be home maybe ten o'clock. I've really gotten interested in that sport. Lots of fun." He gave me a big grin.

"I mean with Mother."

He was instantly furious. Not merely annoyed, but *furious*. "Kelly, just stay out of it," he said fiercely.

"Okay, Daddy, okay. I was just asking. It's my family too."

"Some family," said my father as we pulled in front of the school.

It *was* some family. I had a lovely family. I adored my family. I wanted my family to last. Intact. In love.

I shivered all over. Daddy saw nothing and drove away too fast.

♥

The first three periods of school were torture. You'd think that saying "Hello, Will" to a boy who definitely liked me fell into the realm of the Spanish Inquisition. In my head I said those two words a hundred times, trying to get exactly the right tone.

I dawdled again going to sociology, hiding behind Faith and even Wendy, getting there almost last, sliding into my seat just as Miss Simms was lifting her arm and placing her hand under her elbow. This is perfect, I thought. I get to send Will a quick grin while the rest of the class is getting

126

out paper and pencil, and nobody will notice, and it will still be private and special, but we'll have acknowledged each other.

What a game I was playing.

Too much of a game.

Crazy, I realized. I turned to Will to get past the silliness of game-playing into the real thing.

Will did not look at me.

Then or ever.

He was so tall that staring straight ahead his eyes met nothing but space. He focused nowhere, on no one. Including me.

I couldn't believe it! Hadn't we laughed together? Talked? Understood? Hadn't he had all my chili and half my soda?

Wasn't part of him me and part of me him?

All through sociology I kept turning toward Will. Very slowly, so it would not be obvious to the whole class. It wasn't even obvious to Faith, who was turning toward Angie at the same time.

We're like flowers, Faith and I, I thought.

Turning toward the sun.

Please shine on me.

But Angie was turned inward, and Will was turned away.

Will gave me not one syllable, not one lift of his chin, not one wink, to indicate that we had ever associated, let alone shared any important thoughts or moments.

Halfway through class I stopped trying to catch his eyes. I concentrated on not crying. You jerk, I told myself. Building up a dumb hour over a dumb bowl of chili into a *romance*. It was *nothing*.

13

♥ He didn't call

How could he not call?

It seemed to me we had shared so much, and enjoyed the sharing so much, that he would *have* to call. He couldn't get along with other girls any better, could he? Megan hadn't even gone with him to start with. I didn't know if he had ever done much dating. But surely he would want to date now that we'd had such a nice time at Wendy's!

Apparently not.

The phone didn't ring.

Oh, it rang. Faith, or somebody for Parker.

Faith gave me her usual monologue about wanting Angie to call. I didn't say one word about Will. I still could not share him even with my best friend. Faith wanted the world to tune in to her needs: I wanted nothing. No attention, no sympathy, no understanding.

I just wanted Will.

The week passed.

School was torture.

He greeted me in sociology and history. "Hi, Kell, how are you?" which was more attention than anybody else got. I'd answer, "Fine, thanks, Will." Which was a total lie. I'm surprised my nose didn't get longer. When he had a basketball game in the evening, I'd add, "Good luck in the game tonight."

He'd nod and smile to himself, thinking of the game, not me.

I ran through every sentence we'd exchanged that afternoon to see where I went wrong. If I studied that intensely, I'd be graduating first in my class.

I went to two games.

One against Prospect Hill High. Richie was sitting on the away team's bleachers. Will was getting sweaty and angry, fighting to win, leaping over heads, his sneakers squeaking, his chest heaving. Nothing existed for Will but winning.

And nothing existed for me but Will.

No cheers, no food, no gossip, no other people even.

I knew now what Faith meant about her crush on Angie: a clone of Will was clinging to me, an undercurrent to every thought and motion.

It was like having company that never left: you loved them and hated them for giving you no peace.

♥

Miss Simms okayed the board game for my project. If I really thought I had something, she said, she would show me how to apply for a copyright. I said I didn't really think I had something.

I finished the game on a non-basketball game night.

The board was remarkably pretty. I'd put a lot of effort

129

into decorating and coloring it. Cut and traced a lot of folded paper hearts to get exactly the right sizes for the corners of the poster board. As far as I could tell, the game played well.

But then I knew it by heart.

By heart. Good phrase. I didn't know the game by eyes, or mind or fingertips. I knew it by heart.

It was the way I knew Will too.

By heart.

Each day was the same.

I was either at school or I was home.

I was in the grip of a terrible crush on Will, and he was in the grip of basketball season.

I came home one day to an empty house and found on the table a vase of baby's breath, yellow daisies, and white daisies. My father had tried flowers again. That made me feel slightly better. I walked around the table, staring at the flowers, wishing I had been there when Daddy gave them to Mother. How had she reacted? Had she kissed him? Exclaimed over the flowers? Hugged him and beamed with pleasure? Or shrugged and said, "Put them over there. I'm busy."

I plucked one white daisy and began playing the oldest romance game in the world.

He loves me.

He loves me not.

He loves me.

He loves me not.

For whom was I playing this game? Me and Will? Or Mother and Daddy?

He loves me.

He loves me not.

I could see Will before me, clear as a color portrait. Frozen in space. Or in my heart.

The petals fell on my lap like discarded chances.

He loves me.

He loves me not.

Half plucked, its yellow center became raw on one side, and the stem seemed more fragile. I pulled off two more, counting to myself, and I knew that if I looked at the remaining white petals, my eyes would do an automatic count and I would know the answer.

I averted my eyes.

"Kelly, darling," called my mother, "I'm home."

"Hi, Mother."

She walked into the TV room, saw the vase, the flowers, and the half-picked daisy in my hand. She sat down on the couch beside me, and turned my hand up to look at the pluckings. "What are you on?" she said.

"He loves me."

"Good place to stop. If you keep going, who knows where it might end?"

"There are only two possibilities," I told her.

"When in doubt, it's probably *He loves me not.*"

Oh, don't say it, don't say it, Mother! Tell me that true loves exists! Tell me you are proof. Tell me I will have it too!

"Who is the flower for?" Mother asked.

"Will Reed."

"As in basketball?"

"As in basketball."

Mother nodded, surprised but interested. And then she drew her own daisy out of the bouquet—a yellow one—and my whole stomach clenched with fear. I had this sensation that if she plucked around and ended on *He loves me not,* she would leave. It would all end: their marriage, our family, my life.

But she stared at the flower instead. "I never questioned it before," she said suddenly.

Daddy loving her? "But you always questioned it," I protested. "You always needed him to tell you he loved you."

"I know, but I didn't *really* worry. I just liked to be told. Comforted."

"It's okay to be needy," I said to her suddenly. I thought, *Daddy told me that.* When he was thinking of Mother. That was the only advice he had to give his only daughter. It's okay to need love. You don't have to fight back.

So who was fighting back here? Mother? Daddy? Ellen? Me?

Very slowly Mother slid her yellow daisy back into the bouquet. We weren't going to find out if he loves me or he loves me not. I felt safe. We were still a family: our family, that bouquet—and all of us were still in the water, still alive, still together.

14

♥ *"Because,"* said Faith.

"Because why?"

"Because it's the only excuse we have right now. How else are we going to get both Angie and Will over here?"

I chewed my hair. Bit my fingernails. Twisted my socks and picked at the seam on my jeans. "I can*not* telephone Will and Angie and ask them to come over and play Romance."

We laughed insanely.

"Okay. So you don't tell them what the game is. You explain that you have designed a board game for the sociology class project, and you need to test it. You are throwing a game-testing party. Each person brings a good attitude and a sharpened pencil."

I was getting truly sick of my pink ribcord bedspread. If I got up one more time, looked in the mirror, and saw bedspread lines imbedded in my skin, I would probably set fire to the whole room. "You know," I told Faith, "there's no reason why I can't buy a new spread. Nowhere is it written that I have to live with this pink thing till one of us dies. I've been thinking of a thick soft fluffy comforter in gauzy, flowery patterns. Like clouds of—"

"Stop changing the subject. You're just chicken. Now, are we going to have this party or not? We need to invite twelve people so that we have three sets of players with four apiece."

I raised three fingers and pointed them down my throat.

"Don't gag," said Faith sharply. "This is life, Kelly, and life depends on how you play it."

"You sound like a slogan embroidered on a pillow. 'Life is like a piano, what you get out of it depends on how you play it.'"

Faith grinned. "So we're going to play the game of Romance. And play it to win."

This time I raised four fingers. "Faith, what if nobody wants to come? What if they come, and the sour-cream dip has gone bad and everybody gets food poisoning? What if my mother comes down and behaves weird? What if—"

"Kelly!" screamed Faith, throwing every loose object in my room at my head. "I have sat here all day long making copies of your game! I have colored in yellow flowers and green leaves and pink hearts and scarlet paths! I have drawn lace all around Happily Ever After using my calligraphy set and my special inks! I have lettered *Romance* with Gothic script that twines over the board like lyrics to a love song!" I was ducking perfume bottles, velvet pillows, library books, and packets of false fingernails. "Now, stop fooling around!" shrieked Faith. "We are going to have a party, we are going to invite six boys, and two of them will be Will and Angie, and we are going to play Romance and that's that!"

♥

134

I called Angie first, because I had no stake there.

"Neat," said Angie. "You're so clever, Kelly. Nobody else would be able to design a board game. What's the game about?"

"Secret."

"Oh, and I get to be at the unveiling? I love it. What time? You want me to bring something?"

"Just yourself." I left out the part about the good attitude and the sharpened pencil.

All my calls went like that. Megan was delighted and Kevin Carlson was delighted and Katy Ramseur was delighted and Julie Cietanno absolutely couldn't wait and Mario was surprised and Honey was actually polite. Donny McDonald couldn't get over the idea that I was including him and was I really serious? Did I really want him? Yes, Donny, I really want you.

So I had, including Parker and Faith, ten players signed up. Eager and waiting.

Plus me.

I saved Will for last. (And also for me.) I figured by then I'd have my lines down, and I couldn't goof up the call. Even so, it took about an hour of dialing the first six digits, getting partway through the seventh, and hanging up without letting it ring. Deep breath. Saying to myself, "Kelly, you jerk, *dial the number*. It hardly ever works if you don't dial the number."

"Oh, hi, Kelly," said Will. "I was just thinking about you."

The gift of the century. "You were?"

"Yeah. I'm getting started on my sociology project. I'm just getting organized. Have you given much thought to yours? Listen, I've been so busy with basketball, I haven't had time to eat any four hot-dog snacks let alone make phone calls, but how are you anyway?"

"I'm pretty good," I said, and my heart expanded, filling my whole body, taking up so much space, I felt like a helium balloon rising. Could it be? Just basketball had prevented him from calling? He had thought about me, he would have called, we would have had another four hot-dog snack together—but the coaches wouldn't let him make time? I knew he could have made time. It wasn't the coaches' fault, but I decided to give him one last chance. "As a matter of fact that's why I'm telephoning you, Will. I need special help on my sociology project, and maybe you could come over Saturday night with a bunch of other kids and test it. It's—it takes a group."

"Oh, I'd love to!" He sounded like Donny—he truly would love to. "I'm glad you're including me. What's the project? Do I get a clue ahead of time or is it a secret?"

My throat was so dry, I was croaking. "Secret."

Will laughed. "Okay, I won't push. Mine is not a secret. I'll tell you about mine. I'm a Cummington native, but I'm about the only one I know of. I'm going to find out what percentage of the town was born here, or moved here one year, or five years, or twenty years ago. Who plans to stay and who plans to move on. Statistically correct telephone poll. What do you think?"

"Fascinating," I told him.

"Are you being sarcastic?"

"Only a little."

We both laughed. I said, "I'd love to help with it. How many phone calls will it take? If you wrote out a little script, I could make some for you. That would be loads of fun. We could do it at Megan's house, because they have three phone lines. Make a party of it."

"Megan has three separate phone lines?"

"Yes. A family line, a children's line, and her parents'

business line. If you sit in the office off the kitchen—well, really, it's the dining room, just like my house—anyway, all three phones are on the desk. It would be fun."

"It sure would. Much more fun than sitting alone here and getting all embarrassed every time I try to dial. Great. We'll make it a party. Maybe we should ask Megan first."

We both giggled.

Giggled. Will's laugh was as much a giggle as mine. I loved it. The only thing I wanted more was to be next to him—touching him, seeing him—while we giggled together.

"You want to go over to the library with me this afternoon?" said Will. "I have to go through some town abstracts."

"Sure."

"Great. I'll pick you up in fifteen minutes."

I couldn't stay in the house a whole fifteen minutes: I was no longer a helium balloon floating but some surging, pulsing motor, roaring with excitement, ready to race at top speed. It was as if my crush on Will had rushed through the low gears and gone into high.

I sat outside on the curb. It was raw and nasty out. The stones were like slabs of ice. I sat anyway, watching the traffic stream by. (That is sarcasm. Fox Meadow has about three cars an hour, and they all crawl, because we have so many little children wandering around waiting to be run over.)

Parker suddenly appeared next to me. "Mother is hyperventilating," he said. "I can't stand it. I'm going to freeze my tush out here with you instead."

We sat very close. I don't know if it was the cold or the need. Somehow knowing that Will liked me, that he was on his way, made me strong. Quickly, before I could worry too much about the answer, I said, "Parker, do you think there's more to it than we know? Do you think Mother knows something about Daddy that we don't?"

Parker stiffened and said nothing. I could feel his fear. I could not bear all of us being afraid, holding the fear like a package that could be a bomb, afraid to open it. Maybe it was empty. And if it was a bomb, today it could go off, and I could handle it.

"Do you think Daddy ever had a girlfriend? An affair?"

Parker sucked in his breath. "Kelly, I have to believe he never did. That it's all in Mother. That she's fearful and suspicious and immature."

"But what if he did?"

"Then I think I'd rather not know."

We were holding hands. I could not think of a time my brother and I had ever held hands. It was: *Hold tight enough, we can keep it from being true.*

"I seem to remember you telling Mother that's the ostrich-head-in-the-sand technique," I said softly.

"Yeah, well, the sand is warm under all that sun, you know. A person gets a tan, does a little swimming, listens to the radio, checks out the girls." Park stared into a uniformly gray winter sky. "Guess there's something to be said in favor of sand." Parker sighed and went back into the house.

January.

So cold, and dreary, and even grimy. The very streets and the paint on houses seemed dingy, the way they never would in spring.

Will's car turned slowly into Fox Meadow, past the silly development sign with its gold-leaf foxes playing by the Queen Anne's lace, past the first three houses, which were raised ranches, and on to our section, which were phony Colonials.

I forgot my mother and father. I saw only Will: tall in the seat. His height must be above the waist, for his hair was tousled against the roof of the car, and he ducked down slightly to see us at the curb. I leaped up to go to him and he laughed at my eagerness. With a lunge he yanked open the passenger door for me and stayed down to close it back after I got in.

"That's very athletic," I said to him. "Not everybody can shut a car door on the far side while lying down."

"I'm lying in your lap. It inspired me to Olympic feats."

We laughed. Will circled the development.

Then he circled it again.

"Uh, Will?"

"Right. I'm thinking. Circles are easy decisions."

"What's the tough decision?"

"Where to go? Library or food. I'm incredibly hungry. It was all that stretching over to reach your door. Want to go to Burger King or McDonald's?"

"Once we went to McDonald's," I told him, "and I got all confused over which fast-food place was which, and I ordered a McWhopp."

Will laughed till he cried. "A McWhopp. That's a great name. I think that's what I am: I've eaten so many hamburgers at McDonald's and Burger King and I'm so big that I've turned into a McWhopp."

We went to McDonald's. I had hot apple pie, and Will had two large fries. I guess nutrition wasn't at the top of our list that day.

I began addressing him as McWhopp.

Will put his hands under his chin and stared into my eyes. Slowly he lowered his elbows until he was sprawled all over the tiny table, almost in my face, staring up at me. I looked down into his hair and thought, I cannot possibly tell him we're going to play Romance on Saturday. Or could I? Are we playing Romance right now?

Will asked, "So what is your Saturday-night sociology

139

project?" He winked first his left eye and then his right at me. I can only wink my right. I winked it at him, and he waited for the left to wink, too, but it didn't, so he reached up and very gently squished it into a wink. If I lowered my face, we would be kissing, because he had slid his head all the way beneath mine. I tilted down a half inch.

"Keep going," said Will softly.

I tilted another half inch.

"At this speed of tilt," said Will, "my neck will snap before you arrive."

I tilted the final inch. We didn't actually kiss. Neither of us moved our lips at all. We just touched, and stayed, and felt.

With perfect control Will slid backward. I stayed motionless. Like an eel he slid forward but on a higher level, and this time our noses touched. Our eyes locked. I tilted my face down and he followed, like a dancer. My thin gold hair slid forward and onto his cheek as well as mine, like a veil of gauze, and behind it we touched lips again.

Will sat back instantly. "I love French fries!" he said, and crammed a huge bunch into his mouth. While he chewed he made crazy faces at me with his eyes and eyebrows.

"Okay," he said, "we'll get back to that. It's better in installments, Kelly. Now, tell me how your family is. Are they in divorce court yet? I've been worried about it. Let's get that out of the way, and then we'll have the second installment."

"You're pretty pushy, McWhopp," I said.

He ate more French fries. "Basketball does it to you. Offense, and all that. Come on. Spill it."

I spilled it. Will was a much better listener than Faith, who got so involved that it doubled the anxiety, or Megan, who accused me of things like needing a guide dog for dating.

140

"It's a flimsy marriage," I said finally. "I thought it was all romance. And it's not."

Will shook his head.

"I have to say, Kell, I think it is a very romantic marriage. For your father to accept her insecurity as part of his life, and be nice to your mother about it year in and year out—that is true love. He's willing to make financial, emotional, and time sacrifices for your mother. She could probably use counseling, maybe even psychiatric help. But instead, they used all this romance, and it worked."

"Till now."

"I have a feeling that at dinner with Ellen your father will go out of his way to be terrific with your mother, and keep his arm around her, and open doors for her, and all that."

"But I don't want a wimpy mother," I said.

"Look at it this way. You've got a strong father."

"And what if my mother's view is right? What if he's had an affair, and she has *reason* to be afraid, and the flowers and gifts are all some kind of cheap bribe?"

Will finished the fries. "You're making that up. You aren't basing that on one single piece of evidence, you and Park. You're just trying to justify your mother's behavior. If I were you, I'd rather believe my mother was insecure and dumb than believe my father was out sleeping around."

"I don't want to believe any of it. I don't want it to *be*. I want my family all neat and tidy and loving."

There were eleven French fries left. Will fed me one, ate one, and fed me another one, for eleven French-fry exchanges. "So what's happening Saturday night?" he said.

I let the problem of my parents drop. Gladly. "This winter I developed a board game. You know, like Monopoly. And we're going to try it out."

141

"That is *fantastic*!" he said, and started to laugh.

"Don't laugh at me!" I hissed.

Instantly his face was utterly serious, blank even, and his posture was totally still. "What, me laugh?" he said, as if I had offended him. "I have excellent manners. I never laugh at anybody. Least of all you. That was a warm-up exercise Coach makes us do in practice. Loosens the shoulders." He opened his eyes very very wide, as if to let me in.

"And what is that? A warm-up exercise for your eyelids?"

Will slumped back down, slid across the table eel-fashion again, and came up under my face. "Kelly, you're a mystery to me."

"A mystery? I'm an open book to you. I've told you things I haven't even told Faith."

"*Really?*" Will was immensely pleased. He almost savored that idea. "You've told me things your very best girlfriend doesn't know? I thought girls shared everything. That's one of the things that makes me so nervous about packs of girls."

I could not imagine Will nervous about anything. Could that be what made him seem a snob? Sheer nervousness because girls traveled in packs? How extraordinary! No girl in Cummington High would ever have come up with that explanation.

"Kelly Williams," I said under my breath. "Woman of mystery. I like that, Will. Has a nice ring."

"Yeah," said Will, "well, it's not going to ring of mystery for long. Because I'm going to figure out the score."

15

♥ "Mother!" I screamed. "How *could* you! After I went and swore you to secrecy, you go telling the whole town?"

"It wasn't the whole town. It was just Katy, Kevin, Donny, and Julie."

"I can't stand it! They'll laugh at me. They'll tease me. They won't even come now you've said it's a game of romance. They'll be embarrassed. *I'll* be embarrassed. I'll *die*."

Mother thought that was a bit dramatic. She made faces at me and drove slower. The more she talks and thinks, the slower she drives, so that if she's really involved, you are crawling along, an accident waiting to happen.

"What hour was this?" I said grimly.

"Five maybe. At the mall. I was—"

"It's seven in the evening. All of Cummington knows now that I invented a romance game. By nine o'clock the entire state will know, and by eleven o'clock the national television stations will be preparing a feature."

My mother thought that was pretty neat. After all, if I was going to market Romance nationally, the way Parker wanted me to, it was a good beginning on publicity.

I shuddered. "Turn in here, Mother. You're driving past the pharmacy." Though how anybody could miss an entrance while driving six miles an hour, I don't know.

We entered a vast parking lot. Cummington has several malls, none of which has enough parking except this one. This has eleven times as much as it needs, so there's always a sea of black pavement waiting to be parked on.

The pharmacy was really a general store: everything from closet dividers to picnic baskets. I went to the candy section to find candy hearts. I needed them for players for the game. I had stolen players from my Monopoly set, and Parcheesi and several others, but nothing matched, and there was nothing romantic about them. Then I tried gluing teeny romantic pictures from magazine ads on cardboard, but they were hard to pick up and hard to move over the board. I had colored paper clips and eraser tips but they didn't come in enough colors, and they weren't gamelike; they were desklike.

Then I thought of candy hearts: Valentine's Day specials, in pastel colors with little sayings on them like LUV ME TRULY and BE MINE. I would paint them with clear nail polish and remind people not to eat them and they would be perfect game pieces.

My mother was off looking at Hallmark cards.

I knelt on the dirty linoleum floor in front of the candy and stared down the aisle at her. She fingered card after card. Was she buying Daddy a Valentine's Day card? An apology note? Should I buy Will a Valentine's Day card? A love letter?

Did they have cards that said "I sure hope you love me because if you don't, I'm going to die?"

I knelt there forever, not interrupting Mother, praying

144

she would find a card that said "I love you, sweetheart, let's make up and everything will be the same as before." My knees went to sleep and my ankles hurt. A salesperson appeared to find out if I had died and gone into rigor mortis all over the Valentine's candy.

I bought a very, very large bag of hearts. Now that all Cummington knew, either nobody at all would come to my party or everybody in the world would come.

Mother went to the checkout counter. I staggered to my feet and got in line behind her. "What'd you get?" I said casually.

She showed me her card. A soft photograph, blurred like a watercolor, of two people in a canoe, drifting beneath a weeping willow. It was very very romantic. I opened it, full of hope, and it was blank. "You couldn't find a verse that fit?" I said.

"I think this time I have to write my own."

I thought of all the episodes in my life lately that nobody knew about. Not Mother, not Daddy, not Parker, not Faith, not Megan knew about Will. Parker a little maybe. What episodes in Mother's life did I not know about? What had happened between her and Daddy as they got closer and closer to the reunion and Ellen? Had they called Ellen back? Did Daddy still look at Ellen's letter?

It was amazing that we could live under the same roof, share the same genes and meals and furnace, and lead such separate lives. Glimpsing each other's pain and joy, but sideways, through a window, catching only shadows and reflections, never really being there.

We went back to the car. Nobody was parked around us. Nobody was parked anywhere. It was a marvel the mall was still in business.

"Candy hearts?" said my mother happily. "Oh, perfect, may I tuck a few in with my card?"

My heart, my real heart, soared, thinking of candy hearts. I opened the bag carefully so they wouldn't spill on the car floor and mother picked through them, taking one of each slogan and each color, eating a few, slipping a few in the bag that held her card.

"What are you going to write on your card?" I said.

"No, Kelly." Meaning, Don't ask, it isn't your business.

"Mother, I want to know. You and Daddy are killing Parker and me. What's going on? I hate being a watcher! Wondering! Trying to figure things out. And you two give so few clues. You don't play fair; you keep things bottled and we won't know until it spills. I want to know *now*!"

Mother ate one that said I'M 4 U. After a while she started the motor. She drove slowly out of the parking lot, and slowly into traffic and slowly, dangerously slowly, toward home. She was too filled with thoughts even to press the accelerator. A car behind us honked, and she didn't hear.

"Tell me about it."

Mother found a red light and stopped, which was to her credit. She said, "I don't believe in telling all, Kelly. Some things are better left unsaid."

"But is that a love letter to Daddy? Do you still love him?"

The light was red a long time. When it turned green, it was a long time before Mother moved forward. Two cars honked. She didn't hear either one. "I've always loved your father," she said. "There has never been a minute when I didn't."

And did Daddy always love you? I wanted to ask. But I didn't dare. I didn't want to force her to answer something bad, and I didn't want to hear something bad. I didn't really want details. I just wanted reassurance.

Parker's right, I thought. It's nice to be an ostrich with

your head in the sand. Soak up some rays, listen to the radio, check out the boys. A person can get to like the hot summer sand.

We reached Fox Meadow.

Our driveway.

Mother pressed the button, and the automatic garage door slid silently up. We slid almost silently in, and she turned off the motor. The door closed behind us and we sat in the dim light. My mother put a cool, calm hand over my sweaty, frightened hands and said, "Relax, honey. We had a rough spot, but we handled it. I got by my feelings and Daddy got by his. All is well."

Sometimes with mothers you don't know. You don't have a clue. Are they telling the truth? Or are they being SuperMom and protecting you from pain?

What was the rough spot? Was it real or imagined? Was it Daddy being rough or Mother?

And if all was well now, did it matter? Did I have to know?

"Romance is something you can see," said my mother softly, "like a note tucked under your pillow. Or something you can smell, like perfume or lilacs. Something you can wear, or something you can taste. But love is more subtle, Kelly. You couldn't make a board game of love. It couldn't be contained in little squares."

I sat very still, praying she would tell me, let me be part of it. Whatever it was.

"Love is accepting silence. Accepting apologies. Accepting romance when it's based on love, or grief, or shame, or panic."

The very words terrified me. Flowers? Chocolate? Silver violets on silver chains? Based perhaps on grief or shame or panic?

147

"I love your father. Your father loves me. I made this into quite a storm, Kelly. Almost a hurricane. But we weathered it, all right. And that's all you need to know."

I looked at her profile. I would have been happier if she had faced me to say that. Would have been more sure. It was like a toss of the dice on the board game. Evens, you believe; odds, you don't.

But if love was sometimes accepting silence, then I would accept.

We walked into the house in silence, put away the groceries we'd bought earlier in silence, and I walked upstairs in silence, thinking. Perhaps love is partly silence.

But I walked past the phone, and I knew better.

Love is a telephone that rings for you.

16

♥ The front door opened while Park and I were still setting out the games in the TV room. My mother ran for the door. "Why, Katy!" she cried. "How lovely to see you! Come in!"

Parker and I were squatting across a romance game. "I can't believe you're actually doing this," he muttered. "Setting forth your mind like a menu in front of eleven other people."

"Park, be my helper, not my destroyer."

"I am, I am, I just think you're crazy."

"And Kevin!" cried my mother, loudly so we would hear and come to the door too. "This is going to be such fun. How *are* you?"

"I thought you wanted me to try to sell this game and have it become the newest fad of the nation and be sold in Toys R Us and K mart," I whispered to Parker.

"I do, I do. I just think it would be easier to do it anonymously."

"Romance," I informed him, losing my balance and falling face down into the candy hearts, "is not an anonymous activity."

"Mrs. Williams," cried Katy, matching my mother's tone of voice and certainly returning her hug, "I adore that color on you. Where have you been all winter? You haven't come to a single basketball game. Don't you have any school spirit this year? Shame on you."

Megan came racing across the yard and slammed open the door the way she always does. Angie arrived seconds later. Parker shoveled me out of the candy hearts. "HUG ME is stuck to your cheek," he said.

"Maybe I'll leave it there," I said. "Do you think Will can take a hint?"

Parker groaned. "This romance game is getting to you, Kell." He peeled it off me. "Come on. We have to be host and hostess."

"Donny!" cried my mother. "Oh, my goodness, here come Julie and Will hot on your heels. And Mario and Honey. I guess everybody wants to be on time for Romance."

They all laughed. Slightly hysterical laughter, however.

I walked in ahead of Parker, and everybody giggled at the sight of me and began hugging me. We were all silly and giggly and even with the boys arriving I felt as if this were a girls' junior high slumber party and any minute now we'd start fixing each other's hair and listening to each other's tapes and telling my mother we would pull taffy later, even though we knew we never would.

Katy and Donny and Kevin began guessing what a romance game involved. Kissing? Stripping of clothes? Adding clothes, until we became brides and grooms? Katy asked if we would do an inventory of our hearts.

I liked that phrase.

An inventory of the heart.

As if your heart became an attic, cluttered with trivial crushes and affections but with a few trunks of true love.

Will was grinning at me. His head above the crowd, his eyes fixed my way. What a nice grin he had. The angles and lean lines of his face—like a young Abraham Lincoln—smoothed away and became infectiously happy. He edged toward me, around the other kids. I edged toward him.

We stood next to each other, and I ached to hold his hand, and I would have, too, except that this was the prelude to a romance game. It confused the issue.

Although it was winter, and winter colors are dark, all the girls were wearing pastels. I'm always intrigued when nobody plans in advance, and yet everybody matches. It's like cars on the turnpike driving in clumps, or everybody naming their newborns the same thing. (My birth year it was Jessica; we must have ten Jessicas in our class.) Group telepathy had put the girls in mint-green, pale yellow, and dusty pink. The boys all wore jeans, a shirt with a collar, and a heavy dark pullover sweater with stripes. As if they had known they would need solidarity to play Romance.

Everybody was nervous. "So how do we play this game?" said Angie. His jaw clicked to the side. Perhaps he was afraid of exposing a vein of ignorance.

"First we divide into three groups of four each. Nobody can stay with a girlfriend or boyfriend because it will inhibit you."

Now they really giggled, and pushed lightly into groups, shuffling and poking.

"Wait!" cried my mother. "Don't start yet. Here comes another couple."

Park and I frowned at each other. Everybody was here. Faith and Park and I leaned toward the front window.

Wendy and Jeep.

Crashing my romance party.

What nerve. To come to the home of the boy she just dumped in order to play a game of romance. Which undoubtedly would be *material* for her soap opera.

Wendy bounced up the sidewalk, flirty and gay, with Jeep, handsome and perfect and outshining Parker at her side.

I went to the door to shove them backward into the pricker bushes, but Parker got there first. "Come on in," he said cheerfully. I was so surprised, *I* almost fell into the pricker bushes. "How are you, Jeep? Wen? You almost missed the start of things."

"Give me a break," muttered Faith. "They're *trying* to start things."

Park shot Faith a grin.

The grin caught at me. It wasn't brotherly, the way he usually glanced at Faith. It was a boy exchanging a look with a girl.

Wendy waltzed into the room where she had sat many an evening alone on the sofa with Parker. Did she think this was an act from her soap? Didn't she realize Parker was a real person? That games should stay on the board?

"Do we have room for two more?" demanded Katy, who has always disliked Wendy.

"Any number can play," I said. "I divided us into sets of four because the boards are square and have four sides. But I'll sit out the first game, and Wendy can sit over here with Julie. Jeep, you be over by Angie. We'll just have five at that set."

"We want to sit together," cried Wendy, lip out in a pout.

"Against the rules," said Will. "Boyfriends and girlfriends can't sit at the same board."

Wendy plopped down where I pointed. I gave her the worst possible spot. No support for her back, no place to set a drink or snack, and nobody at the board who liked her. I was happy.

But then the real killer came.

Angie scrunched over to let Jeep sit down, which put him right up against Faith. "Angie," Faith said, flirtatiously, "you can't sit with a girlfriend."

Angie laughed at her joke. "I've never had one. It's not a problem."

The boys dropped to the floor with thuds that shook the lamps on the end tables. Katy and Julie pretended to be shaken by earthquakes, giving shivery little aftershocks and giggling all over again. Faith, for whom it was an earthquake, had tears in her eyes.

And Parker said, "Faith, you and I will be the ones to refill drinks or sharpen pencils."

"Pencils?" said Donny worriedly. "Is this an exam? Do we get graded on how romantic we are? I'm leaving. I'd rather have my teeth drilled."

Parker laughed. "No, this is a great game. You're going to have fun. Trust me." His laugh was real. He laughed into Faith's eyes, and Faith smiled back and he gave her a hug. In a lifetime of being neighbors, Park had given Faith many a thump, scolding, hug, or shove.

But this hug was different.

It was the real thing.

How neat—how positively neat and perfect it would be—to have a romance flower during a romance game. Like the perfect ending.

I wanted to stand and watch, but thirteen people were waiting.

Expecting fun.

I didn't know. Was the game a good one? Would we have fun? I didn't know.

"First, everybody take a pencil and a scorecard," I began. "You have six name slots. Every girl chooses six boy names and every boy chooses six girl names. First names only. I'm going to make the rules different for each group. People at Game One take any old name you like. Say, I might choose Jonathan, Mitch, Jason, David, Lance, and Rob. Or Will might pick Rosemary, Ethel, Maggie, Jessica, Eve, and Wanda."

"Have a heart," said Will. "I don't want to have a romance with a girl named Ethel or Wanda."

"Who *do* you want a romance with?" said Wendy instantly. "Rosemary or Jessica?" Our school is packed with Rosemarys and Jessicas.

"No," said Will. "Somebody named Kelly."

For an instant nobody reacted.

Then it hit: Katy gurgled with laughter, Parker raised his eyebrows, Angie snorted, Donny looked delighted (but then, Donny always looks delighted), and Faith turned all soft and happy for me.

I turned colors and focused on my list of instructions.

Wendy said, "This romance game works fast, Kell. You have drugs in your drinks, maybe? Or hypnotic suggestion in your pencils?"

Parker said, "Only you have to use techniques like that, Wendy. The rest of us have to go by character and personality."

Everybody howled. Wendy didn't take him seriously, because her self-image was so great that she laughs anything off. Jeep didn't defend her; perhaps he agreed with Park, or perhaps he thought it was funny.

Megan said, "Anybody who digs knives into the other players will never never never get to Happily Ever After."

"Is *that* where we're going?" said Will. "I might have guessed." He smiled at me, a private smile, a reference to past talk, and I knew that he was not joking: he wanted his romance with somebody named Kelly.

With me.

After that I could hardly speak. I was so glad I would not be playing the game myself, but going around from group to group making sure their games were working out. Because I didn't want to choose names and have pretend dates and run into Broken Hearts. I wanted to think of Will, and look at Will, and dream of Will, and plan for Will.

"Now this group," I went on, turning to the next set of players, "will choose the six names for the person on your left. That means Katy chooses for Jeep, and so forth."

They nodded and instantly got to work choosing names. Katy said, "Let's see. I'm going to give you a good mix, Jeep. Two sexy names: Jody and Lauri. Two plain names: Catherine and Leigh. And two loser names: Olga and Hortense."

"Just for that I'm giving you Dudley and Percival and Leroy and—"

"But you don't get to choose for me," said Katy with a smirk. "Angie does."

"Don't worry, Katy," said Angie, all smiles like a cherub. "I've got them down. Dudley, Percival, Leroy, and . . ."

I turned to the third group. "You have to choose names of people in your math class in school. No exceptions."

"Oh, no!" screamed Faith. "That's cruel. That's vicious. There are only nine boys in my math class."

"And I'm one," said Kevin. "Make me number three. It's my lucky number. Then you have to put Roy." His voice got singsong and teasing, and Faith moaned piteously. Roy is mean and fat and a druggie and sleeps through most classes, makes ghastly little fourth-grade-boy noises and hasn't washed his hair since junior high.

"I'm taking television and movie stars," said Wendy. "Names from *General Hospital* and stuff. I think I'll put Robert Redford first. He's got blue eyes."

"I have blue eyes," called Jeep. "Put my name down."

"But I know you," said Wendy. "You're against the rules. And I never break rules."

"Just hearts," said Faith softly.

Parker laughed again. "If you're thinking of me, I am wholly mended. Not even a scar to show for it."

Oh, there was so much to think about! Parker over Wendy, Parker and Faith half flirting, Will wanting a romance with me! I hated it that I had to think about this dumb game instead of life. "Turn over your boards," I directed them.

They obeyed.

There before them was my precious game: interlocked hearts, flowers, and the elusive Happily Ever After.

"Everybody choose a player from the pile of candy hearts."

I waited. "Now, the game is played with one die. Each turn you throw twice. The first time, that's the number of spaces you go. So if you roll a three, your player goes three spaces. Roll again. Let's say you get a six. You landed on a Heart space, so you pick up a Heart card. Number six on the card you list under number six on your scorecard. Each of your names will build up a personality and take you on dates from a throw of the die. Everybody see how it works?"

"Oooooh, this is going to be fun!" squealed Katy.

She clapped her hands and demanded to go first at her board and I thought, I *knew* she was the right person to ask.

"Like, sometimes you'll find date number six drives a Porsche, or is a millionaire or is rated medium-sexy," I explained.

"Medium?" repeated Jeep.

"Or you'll find he's got eight hundred zits, or never brushes his teeth, or none of your friends can stand him."

"But I have all movie stars," wailed Wendy. "They don't have zits or forget to brush their teeth."

"That's what *you* know," said Megan. "In this game truth will out."

"Stop talking," said Donny crossly, "I want to play."

"Wait, wait," I said. "I have more directions. The object of the game is to get to Happily Ever After. You have to have at least three dates with somebody to get there. Date spaces have a yellow rose. When you land on a yellow rose, roll the die again, and that's the person you have the date with. It won't work out evenly. Sometimes you never get a date with a person and sometimes you get half a dozen."

"What does it mean when the heart has a streak of lightning through it, Kell?"

They were all reading the board. They were actually getting tense, calculating what was going to happen to this name or that, reaching for the cards to turn them over and see what was in store.

"Broken heart. When you land on a broken heart, you roll your die, and the number you roll has to be struck off your list for good. Even if he's perfect and you've had your three dates and you're in love."

"Oh, no," whimpered Megan. "This is too real, Kell."

"Stop talking," said Donny again. "Let's play."

So they played.

They played Romance, and I stood to the side and watched, and waited for their verdicts.

But I already had the verdict that counted.

Will was on my side.

17

♥ Did any hostess ever have such a successful party?

How many people can dish out love and romance instead of potato chips and Pepsi?

Faith got the terrible Roy, but his personality developed into a wonderful one, until we'd forgotten the real Roy, and were cheering Faith on to Happily Ever After, praying she'd get her third date before she rounded the last heart and headed for Happily Ever After.

Wendy's dates were glorious: they were sexy mountain-climbers who drove expensive cars and took her to exotic places. She went out enough with two of them to reach Happily Ever After—but she landed on Broken Hearts and was out of the game.

Sweet justice.

Parker got a terrific girl named Celeste, but she had one terrible vice: she put him down in public. She was the only one of his six who could go with him to Happily Ever After.

"I can't go there with a girl who puts me down in public!" Parker kept yelling. But he landed on a Lose All Vices square, and Celeste was perfect forever.

"I had a wonderful time, Kelly," said Donny, leaving. "Thanks for including me."

"And me, too," said Katy. "It is such a neat game. I think Parker is absolutely right. You've got to get into New York and sell this thing. It's got potential."

And Wendy, leaving, surprised me. "It's good, Kell," she said without fanfare. "Sometimes you put yourself down. You've got to stop. You're good, your game is good. Go for it. Stop being a wallflower. Get out there and accomplish."

I hugged everybody good-bye.

Will and Faith brought up the rear.

Will was simply nodding at me. "She's right, you know," he said. "Don't like to side with Wendy, but she's right. Go for it."

Are you it? I thought. Are you what I should go for? Or is everybody referring to the game board here?

"How did you do, Will?" said my mother. "Did you fall in love and arrive at Happily Ever After?"

"I didn't progress quite that far," said Will. His eyes never left mine.

What are you saying? I thought, my eyes looking up at his. Are you saying you fell in love? Do you mean me? Do you mean the game?

Don't play games with me, Will.

I want it *real*.

"It's not late," said Will. "You want to go somewhere? I feel like a movie. How about the late late show at Cinema Six?"

"Nobody is going anywhere until the living room is cleaned up," said my father sternly. He appeared so suddenly, we all jumped. "You may not leave this mess for your mother."

I hadn't even noticed the mess, but he was right: popcorn and chips had fallen to the carpet, and empty soda cans and pencils stubs and bowls with nothing left but crumbs were everywhere.

"Kelly and I will clean it up," said Will instantly. "Don't worry about it, Mr. Williams."

Doing anything with Will made me happy. I'll vacuum with you, I thought. Polish tabletops with you. Just stay.

My parents and Faith and Park ambled back into the kitchen. My father was convinced there must be *something* left in the kitchen for him to eat; those teenagers couldn't have consumed every single calorie in the entire house.

We had just filled a paper grocery bag full of trash when my father's voice came down the hall. "I'm wrong. They *did* eat every single calorie."

"But it was such a success, George!" said my mother, laughing. "You've got to play Kelly's game. It's so clever. You'll love it."

"Oooooh, let's play it right now!" cried Faith. "Come on, Park, set up a board. Here, Mr. Williams, I'll pick names for you."

Will swabbed down the piano bench with a damp paper towel. "You mean, your own father doesn't know how your game works?" he said.

"No. I don't think he's been in a very romantic mood lately. I didn't really offer to show it to him. I—I don't know. I'm so afraid I'll jinx something."

"Oh, good, I like him again then," said Will. "I was afraid he didn't want to bother with what his daughter did, and then I wouldn't have any use for him." He gave me a twisted little smile. "On the basketball team three of us have

160

parents who never miss a game. It can be thirty miles away in the hills during a snowstorm, and our parents are there. My parents come, and also my stepparents and usually my *ex*-stepparents. They even sit together. My ex-stepmother is the one who always knows my scores. But some guys—their parents never come. Like Angie. I don't know his parents." Will reflected a moment. "But I know they're no good."

I was staggered. Poor Angie! A mother and father who cared so little for him, they couldn't bother to see him starring in a game? No wonder he was funny with girls. He must not even know what love really is.

I'm lucky, I thought. I know what love is. It hasn't been that sturdy lately—but I know what it is.

And Will, whose parents and stepparents come and go, he knows what love is. They've never stopped loving *him*.

"Yolanda, Emily, and Bunny?" said my father in disbelief. "Faith, let me pick out my own names for this romance."

I stopped tossing paper cups into the garbage bag. Too noisy. What names would Daddy pick? Would one be Ellen? Would one be Violet? Who would go with him to Happily Ever After?

I didn't want my parents to play.

Daddy had hinted that he wanted to be at the party, too, and I was almost rude to him: hinted right back that he wasn't welcome. Because I'm afraid, I thought. They were my standard for romance, and now I don't know. Mother said everything was okay, but I don't know if it is. I certainly haven't seen any proof. The reunion is next week. I don't know how they feel about each other, or about Ellen, or—

"Number one will be Vi," said my father. "Number two, Violet. Number three Viola. Number four—"

"Dad," protested Parker, "you can't do that."

"Why not? I saw you write Faith for your number one."

"Oooooh, did he?" said Faith.

Oooooh, did he? I thought.

Will said, "I wanted to ask you out after we went to Wendy's. I wanted to go out every night. But half the reason I didn't call was basketball. Too busy. The other half was panic, Kelly."

"Panic over *me*?"

"You're very honest, you know. A person has to feel strong to be with you. Boys like Wendy because she sails along, and they get a ride; they don't have to exert themselves."

"I take too much effort?" I thought of myself as the most undemanding girl on earth.

He took my hand and held it different ways, turning it over as if it belonged to him. "You and I started talking about important things maybe five minutes into that date, Kelly. And that's what I've always wanted. A girl who doesn't talk drivel. But when it came, I got panicky. I guess it took me more time than I figured it would to decide to make the effort to really get involved. I kept thinking, *This might count, Will old boy, you'd better be careful.*"

There was only one lamp on in the living room. It cast a soft pool of light. We were in shadow. In the kitchen Parker turned the radio on loudly. He and Faith began singing the hit song that came on, their voices hot and gravelly like the singer's.

I said to Will, "It counted. For me."

We didn't look at each other. We touched instead.

"Okay," said Will. "Okay. Okay."

We both laughed, too softly for the kitchen crowd to hear.

"What does okay mean?" I whispered.

"It means you are putting some demands on me."

"I am not. I am not putting any demands on anybody."

"That's what love *is*," said Will. "Demands."

The radio clicked off midsong. My father, no doubt. He worries about our hearing. He's sure we will be deaf for decades because of the volume of our radios. Daddy said, "I'll tell you what, Faith. Mrs. Williams and I have a little romance game of our own I kind of enjoy. I think we'll play that instead. You and Parker go to the movies with Will and Kelly."

"What a good idea," said Faith.

My mother giggled.

Her own silly, adolescent giggle. Her happy, reassured giggle.

I have to redesign the board, I thought. There's so much I left out! All that I've learned from Will, my parents, Parker, Faith, and even Wendy. But perhaps on a mere board game, there isn't room for even a fraction of what love is.

Will and I sat down slowly on the couch. The garbage bag was still clutched in my left hand, the damp paper towel in Will's. We dropped them to the rug and kissed.

What was a board game compared to that?

"Aaaaah," said my brother. "Come into the living room to find a little privacy of our own and what do we find, Faith? People making out all over the place."

Will laughed.

"Faith and I get the front seat," said Parker. "You two get the back."

"I like the back," said Will.

He and Park grinned at each other. Secret boy-grins. Faith and I hid our grins, but they were there, and oh, how we understood each other then. My crush on Will, and hers on Park, filled the room.

As for my parents, we peeped in on them as we went

out the door. They were hugging. Back where they had been: square one. I liked them in that square. It fit.

"So hurry up already," said Parker. "You can kiss all the way there, but I don't want the movie to start without us."

18

♥ Parker said, "I was on the phone with Wendy all day."

"*Wendy?*" I shrieked. "Parker! I thought you were over her! I thought—"

"Relax. She and I are in charge of raising money for the senior class trip. You know we want to go to Washington, D.C., for four days, and you know we have less than half enough money to do it. Car washes, bake sales, and junior high dances are not going to bring in the heavy cash. And Wendy had a fantastic idea."

Parker put both hands on my shoulders.

Since Will was standing behind me with both *his* hands on my shoulders I felt slightly trapped.

Both boys were laughing: Will pressed into my backbone, Parker into my face.

"I'm a junior," I said. "What do I care about whether your class has the funds to go to Washington? It's *my* class trip I'm worried about."

Parker thought this was very selfish of me. "Listen. Wendy pictured us acting out the board game. Real people paying for tickets to be real players. We'll chalk the board game out on the high school parking lot. We'll set up Romance booths. We'll sell roses. We'll raffle off dinners for two. We'll have hearts circling the high school!" Parker's eyes were sparkling. "We'll make a fortune, Kell! People will pay anything to get romance in their lives."

I gave in.

Who could resist packaging romance like that?

Wendy organized it all. Make a note of this: If you want publicity, choose a girl who loves the sound of her own voice! Wendy got free radio spots and local TV spots because it was so unusual, people wanted to talk about it. We had four newspaper interviews and of course, the usual posters nailed to every telephone pole for twenty miles.

And when the day came, practically the whole town came too: every senior, zillions of giggly junior high kids . . . and all their parents. Who would have thought the game of Romance would be so attractive to grown-ups?

I guess, really, nobody outgrows romance.

More adults than teenagers played.

More husbands than boyfriends bought red roses.

My father helped with the cash drawer, although he resisted at first because the cash drawer was pink and the tablecloth was lace. My mother poured the sodas. Daddy bought her a rose every hour on the hour. She pinned them all to her dress, long stem and all, and she never looked sillier or lovelier.

People walked very carefully around their squares. As if afraid of destroying romance with too heavy feet.

I watched them circle, and laugh, and moan when they hit Broken Hearts and shriek with despair when their best chance acquired some horrid vice.

166

It must have been worth the price of the ticket. Every person who came had fun, and tasted romance, and laughed with his friends. I hoped life would be that good to them: fun and romance and laughter.

"You know, you're going to have to control your face, Kell," said Will. He wrapped both my arms behind me and stuck the stem of a thornless long red rose down my blouse.

"Will!"

"Anybody can look at your face and see you're wondering how much of this chalk on the pavement is a game and how much of it is real."

"Nobody's looking at my face," I told him. "They're all looking at this rose caught in my bra."

Will drew it out, slowly, broke the stem even shorter and fixed it in my hair instead. If it stayed, it would be the first time in my life anything did.

"Come on," said Will. "Let's go over to Happily Ever After and I'll buy you a soda."

We skirted the hearts and shared the soda.

And whether it was Happily Ever After, I wouldn't know for years and years and years. But I was in love with Will and he was in love with me, and the game of Romance went on.

Also available by Caroline B. Cooney

DON'T BLAME THE MUSIC

"I hate you," said Ashley. She spoke softly, intensely, like a hissing snake, and the venom sank into my mother and father. "I will always hate you. I would have been a success if it wasn't for you."

Failed rock star, Ashley, arrives back home after three years of silence – and immediately starts tearing her family apart. Her younger sister, Susan, had been looking forward to an uncomplicated final year at school, but Ashley's outrageous behaviour soon invades every part of her life.

Then Ashley goes too far.

And the family realise they face a desperate and drastic solution . . .

A selected list of titles available from Teens

While every effort is made to keep prices low, it is sometimes necessary to increase prices at short notice. Mandarin Paperbacks reserves the right to show new retail prices on covers which may differ from those previously advertised in the text or elsewhere.

The prices shown below were correct at the time of going to press.

☑	7497 0095 5	**Among Friends**	Caroline B Cooney	£2.99
☐	7497 0145 5	**Through the Nightsea Wall**	Otto Coontz	£2.99
☐	7497 0582 5	**The Promise**	Monica Hughes	£2.99
☐	7497 0171 4	**One Step Beyond**	Pete Johnson	£2.50
☐	7497 0281 8	**The Homeward Bounders**	Diana Wynne Jones	£2.99
☐	7497 0312 1	**The Changeover**	Margaret Mahy	£2.99
☐	7497 0473 X	**Shellshock**	Anthony Masters	£2.99
☐	7497 0323 7	**Silver**	Norma Fox Mazer	£3.50
☐	7497 0325 3	**The Girl of his Dreams**	Harry Mazer	£2.99
☐	7497 0280 X	**Beyond the Labyrinth**	Gillian Rubinstein	£2.50
☐	7497 0558 2	**Frankie's Story**	Catherine Sefton	£2.50
☐	7497 0009 2	**Secret Diary of Adrian Mole**	Sue Townsend	£2.99
☐	7497 0333 4	**Plague 99**	Jean Ure	£2.99
☐	7497 0147 1	**A Walk on the Wild Side**	Robert Westall	£2.99

All these books are available at your bookshop or newsagent, or can be ordered direct from the publisher. Just tick the titles you want and fill in the form below.

Mandarin Paperbacks, Cash Sales Department, PO Box 11, Falmouth, Cornwall TR10 9EN.

Please send cheque or postal order, no currency, for purchase price quoted and allow the following for postage and packing:

UK including BFPO	£1.00 for the first book, 50p for the second and 30p for each additional book ordered to a maximum charge of £3.00.
Overseas including Eire	£2 for the first book, £1.00 for the second and 50p for each additional book thereafter.

NAME (Block letters) ....

ADDRESS ....

....

☐ I enclose my remittance for ....

☐ I wish to pay by Access/Visa Card Number

Expiry Date